Megan felt as if her world dropped away.

Knowing that her parents were dead—and that their bodies rested in the barn—was bad enough. Having this repulsive man tell her more bad news was too much.

"Now, Megan, Mr. Sparks does have a solution to your dilemma." Reverend Porter spoke in the same sonorous tones he used in church. "Mr. Sparks has generously agreed to marry you and take care of the note himself."

Mr. Sparks's grin widened.

Megan felt reality swirling away. "I. . .I can't marry you." Her tongue felt like a huge cotton boll. "I won't." The tremor in her voice lacked the conviction she was hoping to convey.

"Now, Dear." Mrs. Porter patted her shoulder. "I know this has all been a nasty shock, but you can't possibly expect us to leave you in such terrible straits. Mr. Sparks is making a very generous offer. He's willing to take on a new wife. He'll care for your sister, too."

The banker peeled the gloves off his sausagelike fingers and began to unbutton his coat. "I don't believe you have any other choice, young lady. You can't stay out here in the middle of nowhere with no man around to care for you. I'm sure you and your sister will enjoy the amenities that come from living in town."

"He's right." Reverend Porter gestured for his wife to serve the coffee, as though this were his own house and Megan's situation would be readily solved. "Yankton has a lot of young ladies your age. Your sister will be able to attend school. Augustus here has just about the best house in town. Now we can perform the ceremony here, or we can wait until we get back to town. Which will it be?"

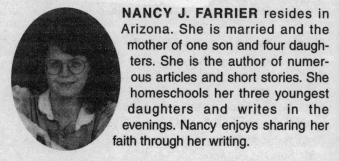

NANCY J. FARRIER resides in Arizona. She is married and the mother of one son and four daughters. She is the author of numerous articles and short stories. She homeschools her three youngest daughters and writes in the evenings. Nancy enjoys sharing her faith through her writing.

Books by Nancy J. Farrier

Don't miss out on any of our super romances. Write to us at the following address for information on our newest releases and club membership.

Heartsong Presents Readers' Service
PO Box 721
Uhrichsville, OH 44683

Or visit www.heartsongpresents.com

Precious Jewels

Nancy J. Farrier

Heartsong Presents

For Hunter, my grandson. He is so precious to me.

A note from the author:
*I love to hear from my readers! You may correspond with me
by writing:*

>   Nancy J. Farrier
>   **Author Relations**
>   **PO Box 719**
>   **Uhrichsville, OH 44683**

ISBN 1-58660-689-1

PRECIOUS JEWELS

All Scripture quotations are taken from the King James Version of
the Bible.

All of the characters and events in this book are fictitious. Any
resemblance to actual persons, living or dead, or to actual events
is purely coincidental.

PRINTED IN THE U.S.A.

one

Dakota Territory—January 1888

Jesse Coulter hunched over in the saddle, clinging to his horse, praying for shelter from the blizzard raging around him. The howling winds tore at him with invisible hands. The cold ripped the very breath from his nostrils.

How long had he been struggling through this storm? It seemed like days, but he knew that couldn't be true. *Oh, God,* he sobbed from his very soul, *I've failed You. I'm so sorry. If I could do it over, I would follow You no matter how difficult. Forgive me, Lord.*

His horse had stopped. He couldn't see, but he could feel the still muscles beneath his hand. He swayed dangerously far to the side. *Tired, I'm so tired.* He could barely form the thought. Then the wind gripped him, lifting his exhausted body into the blackness. The wet snow formed a blanket about him. He felt warmth as the cold fingers of death wormed their way through his sodden clothing. *A whale might have been better, Lord,* he thought as the blackness closed about him.

❧

Megan Riley paused, her mittened hand resting on the door latch. Rising panic tightened her chest, making breathing difficult. She leaned her head against the door, listening to the gale outside trying to tear the house apart. *Where are they? Why aren't they home by now?* Tears she couldn't afford to shed if she were to go out in the frigid weather threatened to fall anyway.

She glanced at the curtain blocking her view of the bed she

5

shared with her younger sister, Seana. Indecision reigned. As the outside temperature dropped through the day, Seana's fever had risen, then broken at last. She finally slept, but Megan felt a desperate need for their mother to be here.

"Meggie."

A sudden drop in the wind brought the hoarsely whispered word to Megan. She quickly crossed the room and opened the curtain. "What is it? I thought you were asleep."

"Is Momma home?" Seana's pale face gleamed in the lamplight. "Where are you going?"

"Hush, now. There's no need to worry. Pa probably decided to stay in town rather than head home today. Maybe he and Matt didn't get everything loaded in time. They're most likely still visiting with Pastor and Mrs. Porter. You just rest. I'm going outside for a little more firewood."

Megan watched her sister's dull gaze drift to the pile of wood along the inside wall. "But you've brought in enough wood, haven't you?" The soft words were full of fear.

"I suppose I have." Megan smoothed the hair from her sister's forehead. "But for some reason I feel the need to bring more."

Seana closed her eyes. "You're right, Meggie. I feel it, too. Hurry back." Her head turned on the pillow; her eyes closed again in sleep.

Megan swallowed against the lump in her throat. *God, please take care of her until I get back. Help me to be safe.* At nine, Seana was eleven years younger than Megan. She had followed Megan since she could first toddle on unsteady legs, always calling her Meggie.

Outside, the wind, a howling banshee determined to have its way, pushed Megan back against the side of the house. The bitter cold burned all the way down her chest as she breathed in. She adjusted her scarf to cover her nose, hoping it would warm the air a little. Tiny needles of snow did their best to pierce the few parts of her face exposed to its touch.

Megan groped for the wood sled, thankful once more that her father had made it. On snowy days, it was so much easier to pull a sled full of wood than to carry an armful of logs while crossing the treacherous ground. She fumbled for the rope that would guide her through the storm and growing darkness. Earlier this afternoon she had put up a guide rope to the barn and to the woodshed so she wouldn't get lost.

The heavy drifts resisted her efforts to move. Her feet felt like lead weights after only a few steps. *God, I don't know why You have me doing this, but please help me. A person could easily freeze to death in this. Keep me safe. And, Lord, please keep Momma and Papa and Matt safe. I don't really think they stayed in Yankton another day. This storm began so suddenly, they could have been caught unaware. I don't think they were prepared for it to get this cold. Please watch over them.*

Tucking her head down to block the arctic air, Megan plowed ahead. Used to the resisting tug of the snow, she didn't realize her foot had connected with something solid until it was too late. She lost her grip on the lifeline and tumbled forward into the snowdrift, freezing ice crystals coating her face. She braced for the impact, a jolt of surprise racing through her as her hands contacted something that didn't belong in the deep snow.

A bump against her shoulder knocked Megan sideways. She stifled a scream that wouldn't be heard in this howling gale anyway. She lifted her head, squinting to see in the dimness of the late afternoon. She saw the movement just before the horse's nose nuzzled against her shoulder. Heart pounding, she reached up to pat it, then bent to brush aside the snow at her feet.

Whose horse was this? Had her father or Matt ridden ahead? Had she stumbled over one of them? Frantically, she dug, blindly seeking whomever lay buried here. Ever so slowly, she managed to free the upper body from the snow. *God, help me! I can't do this on my own. How will I ever get him inside? I'm not strong enough, and the snow blows back as fast as I push it away.*

Calm began to replace the panic. Megan knew she had to think clearly or whomever this was would die before she could help him. She inched upright, patting the horse that stood so close it blocked a bit of the wind. A tug on her arm reminded her of her errand. The wood sled. Of course! If she could only get him on the sled, she could pull him to the house.

Megan hauled the long sled next to the inert body. *God, please don't let him be dead!* She yanked and struggled, wondering how her little bit of strength could move someone so heavy. She knew for certain this wasn't her father or Matt. They were both slightly built, and this man—for she was sure it was a man—had much broader shoulders. In fact, his stocky body was proving impossible to lift onto the sled.

God, he's going to die if I don't get him inside. Please, help me.

The horse leaned over and blew its warm breath in her face. Megan brushed the ice crystals from the horse's nose. She gasped as an idea dawned, then doubled over in pain as the cold air rushed down her throat. Straightening, Megan began to run her hands down the horse's neck. Frantically, she prayed to find what she needed.

Relief flowed through her as her hands connected with a circle of rope. She fumbled with the leather thong while tying it to the saddle, wishing she could take off her awkward mittens. The rope finally dropped into her hand, and she quickly tied one end securely to the pommel.

She knelt next to the man, brushing away drifting snow that accumulated in the last few minutes. Making a second loop, she seesawed it over his shoulders and under his arms. Pulling it tight, she stood and groped for the guideline. She sighed with relief as her fingers connected with her lifeline to the house.

Snow swirled; darkness marched closer. Megan realized she had no idea which way the house was. In the midst of trying to rescue this man, she had gotten turned around. She spun one way, then the other, straining to see through the raging blizzard. Panic washed over her like a wave.

Think, Megan, a nearly audible voice spoke. *Remember where you were at the start.*

She dropped back into the snow beside the man. Her thoughts scrambled, and she tried to remember exactly where she had been when she first found him. She closed her eyes and peace crept over her. *On his right side. Yes, that was it.* Megan stood, grasped the rope, and began to lead the horse toward the cabin.

The door resisted her momentarily, as the wind pushed to keep it closed. Then, when she despaired of getting it open, the wind gusted a different way, and the door swung wide. Megan slipped in amid a swirl of snowflakes, leading the horse.

"Whoa." She patted the horse's neck as she unfastened the rope from its saddle. "Easy, now. I'll put you in the barn as soon as I take care of your rider."

The horse filled half the small room. Megan edged past him, hoping he wouldn't get feisty in the cramped space. She dragged the stranger farther into the room and swung the door closed, shutting out the nasty weather.

"Meggie, there's a horse in our house." Seana's awe-filled voice was nearly lost in the noise of the horse's whicker.

"Seana, what are you doing out of bed?" Megan looked over at her wide-eyed sister. "I know there's a horse here. I had to use him to bring this man in before he froze completely. Now go hop in bed. I have work to do."

"But Meggie, who is that? Did Papa come home?"

"No, it's not Papa. It isn't Matt, either," Megan said, anticipating the next question. "I don't know who it is. I found him in a snowdrift outside. I don't even know if he's alive."

Megan glanced up at Seana's gasp. She regretted her harsh words, but couldn't take them back. She slipped her fingers under the man's coat collar. "I'm sorry, Honey. I shouldn't have said that. He is alive. I can feel a pulse, although it's a little weak."

Megan stood and ducked under the horse's neck. She leaned over and gave Seana a quick kiss on her cool cheek. "You've just gotten over your fever, and I don't want you to get worse. Please get back in bed. I'll get this man over by the fire where he can warm up, then I'll come tell you all about it."

She turned to duck past the horse again. Puddles of melted snow were building around his feet and steam rose from his coat, filling the room with the rank smell of wet horsehide. "Come to think of it, I think I'll take the horse to the barn before I check on you."

As Seana disappeared behind the divider, Megan turned to the task of dragging the man closer to the fire. Once there, she set about removing his wet outer clothing. She brought dry towels and rubbed the snow from his face and hair. She tried to ignore the wide set of his shoulders, the strength of his arms, and the strange feelings inside her. His rugged, sun-brown complexion told her he spent plenty of time outdoors; but his smooth hands said it wasn't at hard, physical labor.

Drying his hair, she felt a lump the size of an egg on the side of his head. "You must have hit your head when you fell off your horse." Megan didn't know why she spoke the words aloud.

His full lips turned up, twitching his mustache. His eyelids fluttered. Megan found herself staring into a pair of eyes the color of the cinnamon sticks Momma grated for cookies.

His smooth-fingered hand brushed her cheek. "Angel," he whispered hoarsely. "You're my angel."

His hand fell and his eyes closed once again. Megan touched the place where his hand had been. Never had she felt anything like this.

two

In the dim lantern light, Megan's frost-numbed fingers struggled to loosen the cinch. Eerie shadows danced across the stable wall. The buckskin dipped his brown nose in the pile of sweet hay she had thrown in the feeder. For tonight he could have one of the stalls usually reserved for her father's horses. She leaned wearily against the horse's tawny side. Her legs trembled as she listened to the howling wind and felt the biting cold. Were her parents and brother out in this storm? Had they stayed in Yankton with friends? Where were they?

Plucking a handful of straw, Megan began to rub the tiny bits of ice from the horse. Grunting, as if in appreciation of the attention, the steed leaned heavily against her hand. His tail swished, flicking her exposed cheek with its wet strands.

"I'm not a fly you have to swat." She gave his flank a light smack. "I wish you could tell me a little of your master. Where were you heading that you ended up on our doorstep?" She sighed and patted his neck. Dumping a small amount of grain in with the hay, she hefted the saddlebags and lantern. Pulling her mittens back on, she adjusted her scarf to cover her face, steeling herself to fight her way through the cutting wind.

God, please help this storm to be over by morning. I know worry is a sin, but I can't help it. I want to know my family is safe, but deep down I feel like something isn't quite right.

The cold, wet flakes of snow stung her eyes as she stepped from the barn's shelter. The wind battered her back against the door, slamming it shut. Throwing the saddlebags over her shoulder, she groped through blinding snow until she found the rope that led to the house. *Only a little ways,* she assured herself. *I can do it. Seana needs me, and so does that man.*

After what seemed like hours, she pushed open the door of the cabin and stumbled into the cheery warmth. The stench of wet horse had faded; the floor would probably dry by morning. Setting down her burden, she stripped off her icy outer clothes and hung them on pegs near the door.

The stranger lay still as death near the fire. She stared at him, feeling the rise and fall of her own breathing as she willed his chest to move likewise, relief flooding through her as she detected the slight motion. Turning, she crossed to Seana's room. *Oh, please, I don't think I could cope with a dead man on top of everything else that's happened. Help him live, Lord,* she prayed silently, realizing that it was a selfish thing to pray.

Megan touched Seana's brow, and Seana opened her eyes. "Momma?"

Megan winced at the scratchy sound. "No, Seana, it's Meggie."

"Where's Momma?" Tears welled up in Seana's eyes. "I want Momma to sing to me. When will she be home?" Megan smoothed her hand over Seana's forehead, wondering how she could soothe her sister's fears when she had so many of her own. "Momma and Papa haven't come home yet. Perhaps they've had to stay in town another day. If they suspected the storm was coming, I'm sure they would have stayed over."

"But I want Momma." Seana began to sob. "Please make her come home."

Tears stung Megan's eyes. Seana rarely cried or demanded her way. That she was doing so now only spoke of her sister's fear.

"Will you sing to me, Meggie?"

"Of course." Megan smoothed her sister's hair and began to croon their mother's favorite song. Seana's eyelids fluttered, then slowly drifted shut. Megan continued to sing until her sister's breathing deepened and she slept.

Back in the main room, she dug her fists into the small of her back to ease the ache from leaning forward for so long. A low moan beckoned to her from near the fireplace. Crossing the room, she knelt beside the stranger.

"What am I supposed to do with you?" She didn't expect an answer. "You need to be up off the floor, but I know I can't move you by myself."

She studied the man on her floor. He reminded her of the broad and sturdy oxen her father kept for plowing the fields. She smoothed back the toffee-colored hair from his face. He needed a trim in both his hair and his mustache, the latter an interesting blend of reds, golds, and browns.

I don't know why I care what you look like. I know God doesn't intend for me to marry. If He had, He would have made me a lot more appealing. There isn't a man around who would look twice at me.

Laying the back of her hand against his forehead, Megan checked for fever. "I don't know why I did that. I have no reason to believe you're sick. Most likely it's the lump on your head and the hours of exposure that are keeping you asleep." She sat back on her heels and frowned. "Although, if I don't find a way to get you off the floor and in bed, it's quite likely you will end up sick."

As if in answer, his eyes snapped open. His panic-stricken gaze swept the unfamiliar surroundings before coming to rest on Megan's face. For a long moment, his warm cinnamon eyes stared at her.

"Angel," he whispered hoarsely. "I'm sorry. I couldn't stay with her. It would have been wrong. I had to go or I would have hurt her worse than I did. Please tell me you don't hate me for it."

His eyes closed, and she thought he'd lapsed back into

sleep. Then, eyes still closed, his hand stretched upward until his fingers brushed her cheek. She took his hand and tugged gently, wondering if, with his help, she could get him to her parents' bed. Like a sleepwalker, he stood and allowed her to lead him. Within moments, she had him tucked beneath warm quilts. As she turned to go, his hand wrapped around her wrist. Her heart hammered as she pulled against his soft grip.

His eyes flickered open, then closed. "Sara, I didn't mean to hurt you." His grip relaxed, and he closed his eyes in sleep.

Megan touched her cheek where she could still feel the brush of his fingers. He'd called her Angel. *It must be the bump on the head. Angels are beautiful. No one in his right mind would ever confuse me with an angel.*

The angel faded and Jesse labored up the hill on leaden legs. "Sara, wait." Each step took more energy than he thought he had. He gasped for breath, his lungs burning. Sara, her red-gold hair floating around her like a mantle, beckoned him from the top of the hill. Her tinkling laughter echoed across the fields.

"We must talk." He yelled as loud as he could, yet he knew it wasn't enough. The thick air grasped at him, slowing his progress.

Sara clapped her hands impatiently. The hill faded, and he stood before Sara's house. The street was lined with carriages and horses. People milled about the yard. As he strode toward the door, men moved to pound him on the back, and women smiled and giggled.

A feeling of dread settled in the pit of his stomach. He looked up to see Sara framed in the doorway. Captivating Sara. From the wealthiest family in town. This was his engagement party. He was the envy of all the young men around. He had everything going for him. No one else knew how he would break her heart.

"Sara, we have to talk." He shouted to be heard above the crowd. "I have to explain." People were staring at him. Sara gave a petulant frown and beckoned him to come closer. He backed toward the gate. "It isn't right, Sara. It won't work."

He ran. Anguish ripped at his soul. He had to escape. The faces of his family and friends flashed by. They all tried to voice their disapproval. Hands reached out to stop him, but he ran on. The town faded in the distance. Another voice called, beckoning him to follow. But he hurried on.

"You don't understand," Jesse shouted to the hills. "I don't want what she wants. I'm not the person she expects me to be. God, I'm not who You want me to be. I can't do it." A sob tore from his throat. "I'm a simple person."

He fell to the ground. The soft grass waved around him. The scent of summer faded and the warmth turned to a chill that crept into his bones. Snow raged. The tiny flakes became daggers piercing his skin over and over.

"Oh, God." Sobs tore at his chest. "I'm not worthy to follow You. I can't do it on my own. Please, if You want me to follow You, then give me a wife willing to stay beside me when I falter. Help her to love You enough to encourage me. Help me, God."

Peace settled over him. The dream faded and he rested, sleeping deep for the first time in weeks. He wrapped the heavy quilts close, sighing in contentment.

The voice of an angel murmured at his consciousness. The sweet melody wove a spell around him, pulling him awake. He forced his eyelids up and regretted it immediately. His eyes felt as if someone had thrown a bucket of sand in them. He closed them, wishing for cleansing tears that never came. Instead, the heavenly music spun about the room on a magic thread. He drifted to sleep again, wondering if all heaven's angels sang like this one.

He stood in his father's study.

"What are you doing with your life, Jesse?" His father's stern tone startled him.

Jesse glanced around. The huge mahogany desk only emphasized his father's imposing stature. Sunshine coming in the windows glinted off the polished paneling. The thick carpet muffled his footsteps as he neared the desk, placing his hands on the back of one of the overstuffed chairs facing his father.

"I'm going to work in the mine fields." He tried to sound determined.

"What about your marriage to Sara?"

"She isn't right for me." His hands gripped the chair, feeling the smooth leather give beneath his fingers.

"You're giving up a secure future to follow some gold lust?" His father's angry roar rattled the window glass.

"I can't stay here and be forced into a mold where I don't fit. Sara and I would both be miserable."

"I'd say the young lady is miserable right now," Richard Coulter thundered at his son. "You're not only bringing shame to her, you're disgracing our family name."

"I'm sorry." Jesse tried to find the words to make it right.

Jesse heard a sniffle and turned to the door. His mother stood there, her perfectly coifed blond hair a contrast to the dark surroundings.

"We need you here, Jesse." She pressed a bit of lace to her nose. "How will we ever get by if you leave?"

The room faded. He started to stretch out his hand, then stopped. "God will take care of you, Mother," he whispered. "He'll watch over you when I'm not here."

The angel's soft melody drifted near, her voice weaving around his very heart. Jesse tried once again to open his eyes. The light was dim, but he could see a figure hovering near him. Was this heaven?

His angel leaned close. Blue-gray eyes, sparkling with life, gazed at him. She wasn't beautiful, but an earthy prettiness warmed him to her. She smiled, and he tried to lift his heavy hand to touch the dimple in her left cheek. His body wouldn't respond, and he drifted away again. Was the angel real or simply another figment of his tormented dreams?

three

Streaks of sunlight fought a losing battle with the cold of the room when Jesse woke again. Motes of dust swirled in the air. A small fire crackled in the hearth.

His head throbbed, but at least he could think now. Jesse gave the room a slow perusal. The bed stood close to the wall, an armoire and table with a washstand near the closed door. Lifting his head, he tried to discover why he couldn't move. Weights seemed to be attached to his body, holding him in place; however, he couldn't see them. His head dropped back against the pillow, a film of sweat covering him from the exertion. He gasped for air, every breath sending needles of pain through his chest.

The door creaked, the scent of fresh-baked bread and stew making his stomach growl. Turning his head, he could see a pixie face peeking around the door frame. The girl stared at him, a look of surprise on her pale features. One long brown braid swung like a pendulum in front of her shoulder, the only movement in a frozen tableau. She jerked back. The door slammed shut. He could hear her crying out, but couldn't make out the words.

The door swung open again. This time the young girl rushed into the room, tugging on the hand of a young woman. Jesse had vague memories of seeing her face. He tried to push up. Sweat beaded on his skin. A chill swept over him.

"See, Meggie, I told you he was awake." The pixie's braids bounced as she clapped her hands in delight.

"Calm down, Seana. I don't want you to have a relapse." Meggie moved over to the bed, where Jesse could get a good look at her. A neat coil of dark brown braids framed her round face. She leaned over to touch his forehead, her blue-gray eyes full of concern. The light in the room seemed to surround her when she smiled. His angel. He'd thought he'd been dreaming, but she was real.

"How are you feeling, Mr. Coulter?" Her fingertips grazed his forehead. Her dimple faded as she frowned at him. "You feel awfully warm. Are you hot?"

"No, Ma'am." His voice sounded scratchy from disuse. His body throbbed. He wanted nothing more than to fall asleep again. Another chill coursed through him. Jesse thought about asking for another blanket, but the effort would be too much.

Sleep weighed him down. He fought the tug of it, wanting to ask how she knew his name. Did he know these people? How had he gotten in this bed? What was wrong with him? As if through a hollow tunnel, he heard Meggie talking to the young girl.

"Seana, fetch me a rag and some cool water. Quick. Mr. Coulter is running a fever." The covers over him were loosened. Cool air rushed across his neck, and he shook with the chill. Something pressed against his chest.

"Seana, slow down, you're spilling the water."

"What's the matter with him now, Meggie?"

"I'm afraid he might be getting pneumonia from being in the snow and cold for so long. His breathing is congested. We'll have to fix something so he can breathe easier."

Jesse remembered the snow now. Darkness closed in tighter. The weight on his chest pressed down, robbing him of the precious air he needed.

⁂

Megan worked at a feverish pace. She had Seana bathing Mr. Coulter's face with cool water, while she peeled and sliced onions to make a poultice. Last winter her brother, Matt, had gotten pneumonia. She'd helped fight the sickness with her mother and could still recall the various remedies they'd used.

"Meggie, why are you crying?" Seana looked tired as she

came out of their parents' bedroom. Megan wiped her cheeks on her apron.

"I'm peeling onions, Seana. They always make me cry."

"Momma always cries, too." Seana's voice got very soft. Megan could hear the tears her sister struggled to hold back. She, too, had been praying once more for her parents and brother. Although she hadn't lied to Seana, the tears weren't all from the onions. Her heart ached with the fear that something had happened to her family.

For two days now, the storm had raged. Only by staying in town could her family have come through this blizzard unscathed. Even if the snow stopped now, it would be another two to three days before anyone could hope to get here from Yankton. The drifts would be too deep to get through. Her parents had the wagon, not the sleigh. Somehow, she had to distract Seana and keep her from worrying. Seana had never been strong. Megan hated to think how her sister would react if something bad were to happen to their parents.

"Do you need more water for Mr. Coulter?" Megan pasted on a smile.

"I didn't know if I should keep using the cool water. He stopped sweating and now his teeth are chattering." Seana set the empty bowl on the table. She wrinkled her nose as she leaned over the skillet of onions. "Are you making that evil-smelling poultice that Momma made for Matt?"

"Yes. I'd appreciate you not calling it evil smelling." Megan's lips twitched as she recalled those very words coming from her father's mouth last year.

"Papa said Momma stunk up the whole countryside." Seana's blue eyes were wide as she gazed up at Megan. "He said the crops would have died if Matt hadn't gotten well in time."

Megan chuckled. "Papa was just joking. The fumes from these onions will help Mr. Coulter to breathe. He's having trouble getting air. That's why his breathing is so loud."

"Will he die?"

Megan felt like someone had rubbed her face in the snow. She wanted to yell at Seana and tell her not to ask such a ridiculous question, but she knew she'd been wondering the very same thing. "We'll pray that he doesn't." She hugged Seana. "You know Momma always claimed Matt got well more from the prayers than from the medicines she gave him."

"Then let's go right in and pray for Mr. Coulter." Seana grabbed Megan's arm. Megan laughed.

"You need to rest first, and I have to finish this poultice." She couldn't help noticing the way Seana's freckles stood out against the paleness of her skin. "You go lie down. I'll get these onions cooking and then go pray for Mr. Coulter. When you get up, we'll pray for him together. Okay?"

Seana nodded. "Will he get mad at you?"

"Mad at me for what?"

"Because you looked through his saddlebags."

Megan sighed. "I hope not. I needed to find out who he is." She didn't want to tell Seana she'd been looking for someone to contact if the man died. Megan hadn't thought he would live through the first night. Now, with pneumonia setting in on top of his injury and exposure to the cold, she didn't know what the outcome would be. How she wished her parents were here. They would know what to do.

Throughout the night, Megan sat by Mr. Coulter, alternately using the cool cloth to bring down his fever and changing the onion poultice. As the hours passed, she thought his breathing eased, but she couldn't tell for sure. If so, the change was slight. He continued to labor at drawing in air. One moment he would be sweating and throwing off the covers. The next moment his teeth would start to chatter, and he would shiver from the chills running through him.

Megan prayed harder than she'd prayed for anyone or anything. Last year when Matt had been so sick, she'd asked God to heal him, but not with the fervency she did for this stranger. After all, both of her parents were praying for Matt. This time only Seana's sporadic prayers were added to hers.

"Meggie?" Seana's soft words drifted through the thick fog of sleep surrounding Megan. She lifted her head and blinked. She'd fallen asleep with her head resting on the bed beside Mr. Coulter.

"Meggie, he's still alive. I hear him breathing." Seana looked like a waif in her nightgown.

Surging up, Megan groaned at the ache in her back from the unusual position she'd slept in. Lifting the covers, she yanked off the cooled poultice. How could she have fallen asleep and left this to grow cold? She shook her head to clear the cobwebs and placed her ear to his chest. If the congestion had lessened, she couldn't tell. He still labored painfully to pull in the air he needed.

"We'll have to heat up some broth and try to get him to take a few sips, Seana. He can't fight this sickness if he is weak from lack of food. Why don't you help me with breakfast while the broth heats?" She held out a hand to her sister.

By the time Seana finished eating, the broth was warm. Megan managed to rouse Mr. Coulter enough to get him to swallow a few spoonfuls. Then he collapsed against the pillow, eyes closed, the sound of his struggle to breathe filling the room.

Megan thought he was asleep again. As she tucked the covers close around him, his hand shot out and grabbed her arm. His slitted eyes stared at her. "Sara, I can't do this. You have to let me go. Why do you keep following me?" He began to cough hard enough to shake the whole bed.

Eyes wide as saucers, Seana watched from near the door. Megan tugged at her arm, trying to break free from his tight hold. The coughing spell ended, leaving him weak and shaking.

"Sara, please, I have to leave." He gasped out the words.

"It's okay. You can go." Megan held her breath as he froze, watching her with glazed eyes. His grip loosened. She pulled free. His whole body relaxed, and he slept again. Megan covered him before turning to leave.

"Meggie?" Tears were running down Seana's cheeks. Megan hurried to her sister and hugged her.

"What's the matter?"

"I thought he would hurt you. I was so scared." Seana clung to Megan, her body shaking. Megan herded her sister out of the bedroom and closed the door.

"Sometimes when people are very sick, Seana, they see things that aren't there. Mr. Coulter must have thought I was this Sara whom he knows."

"Who is Sara?"

"I don't know. I only found his Bible in his saddlebags. His name was written in there, but he'd recorded nothing else. When he wakes up, he'll tell us about this Sara if he wants us to know."

Megan sank into her mother's rocking chair and lifted Seana onto her lap. The rhythmic movement soothed them both. Seana, small for her age due to all the sickness that plagued her, seemed to weigh nothing at all. Her head rested on Megan's shoulder just as Megan had seen her rest against her mother many times. In no time Seana's deep, even breathing told Megan her sister had fallen asleep. She had so much to do; but for a few minutes longer, she relished the feel of her sister and the comforting motion of the rocker.

❧

Jesse drifted in a cloud of pain. Voices swirled around him, some making sense, others only a distracting noise. Through it all, the heavy weight continued to press down on him like rocks piled on one by one. He didn't know how much time had passed. He couldn't tell whether it had been days or hours since this pain enveloped him. Somehow time didn't matter, only the battle at hand: the battle for his life.

"You have to marry Sara. She'll be the one to bring this family into the society we deserve. It's your duty to us, Son." His father's stern tones rumbled through Jesse's head. Society had always been the unattainable carrot his father strove to reach. All his life Jesse had been schooled to marry right so they would have the name and fortune needed to propel them forward. He'd failed, and his father would never forgive him.

"Jesse, Dear, you simply must give up this infatuation with religion. It isn't fashionable to be so fanatic about God." His mother's dulcet voice rang in his ears. *"Attending the right church is important to one's place, but you needn't run around talking about Jesus as if He's a friend to you. People will think you're a lunatic."* He could see his mother smoothing her perfectly coifed hair as she prepared to attend another tea, wearing the latest fashion, acting as haughty as any society matron. She tried to hide her disappointment in him, but Jesse knew he could never live up to her standards.

"If you truly love me, you'll give up this silly idea of going to the gold fields in Dakota Territory." Sara gave a pretty pout as she twirled her parasol, the whirling colors as mesmerizing as a snake. *"You don't want to go to such a dirty place when you can be here with me."* She smiled and pursed her lips, tempting him with all she offered. The day he left her, she vowed to get him back one way or another. She would carry a grudge until the day she got her way.

More rocks were piled on him. Jesse strove for a breath; the weight on his chest made the drawing in of air almost impossible. Spikes of pain tore through him with each effort. *Jesus, help me.* His tormented cry brought to mind the scene of his Savior on the cross, struggling to push against the nails so He could breathe. Jesus knew his suffering. He'd endured worse.

Tears burned in Jesse's eyes. *Please, Lord, give me another chance to serve You. I'll go anywhere You ask, even home.*

The darkness lightened. The boulders on his chest warmed. Heat spread through his body, helping him to relax. He felt as if the hand of God was touching him, easing his hurt, changing his life. Relaxing as the agony lightened, Jesse drifted closer to the light.

Murmured words wove through his consciousness. Someone was in the room with him, talking. He wanted to turn back to the darkness. He couldn't face disappointing someone else. The promise he'd just made to God drifted through his mind. How could he have forgotten so soon? This was the direction God was leading him. He had to trust.

"Jesus, please, I don't know what to do for him anymore. I don't know what Seana will do if he dies. I don't know what I'll do." The sound of a woman crying compelled Jesse to awaken. His eyelids were so heavy as he forced them up. The flickering light of a lamp made him blink. Tears welled up, trickling down his cheeks. He couldn't move to stop them.

He'd never been so tired, yet Jesse knew without a doubt he'd been healed. Trying to draw in a deeper breath, he set off a spasm of coughing. Spikes drove through his lungs, but he'd gotten enough air to know he could breathe better.

"Meggie, look."

The coughing fit eased. Jesse saw the pixie in the doorway staring at him. He rolled back over to see his angel rising from a kneeling position by his bed. She'd been praying for him. He stared at her, concentrating on taking shallow breaths so he wouldn't cough again.

"Meggie, will he live?"

His angel nodded. "I think so, Seana." Her touch to his forehead felt like the flutter of butterfly wings. Jesse couldn't tear his gaze from her. He wished he had the strength to return her touch.

four

Frigid air brushed his cheeks when Jesse woke the next morning. Embers smoldered in the fireplace. His breath puffed out in white clouds. Under the pile of blankets and comforters, he stayed warm. For the first time since arriving here, he wasn't too hot or too cold. Although his body still felt the heavy weight of exhaustion, he could draw in shallow breaths without pain.

The door swung open. The woman he'd seen earlier entered, her arms piled with wood for the fire. She glanced at the bed and froze. "Oh, I didn't think you would be awake. I'm sorry." Her cheeks reddened as she stared at the floor. "I would have knocked first, but you have been asleep so long."

"I just woke up. Go ahead." The effort to speak left him gasping. Racking coughs began to shake his body. He curled on his side, trying to hold his breath to stop the coughing. By the time he could breathe again, the woman had the fire going and stood over him, one hand slapping against his back. Jesse had never been so tired.

"When my brother, Matt, had pneumonia, he would cough like this. Momma said he needed to get rid of the congestion clogging his lungs." The woman backed away. "I'm guessing that's what you need to do, too."

He tried to speak, but she held up her hand. "Don't. Talking will only make you cough again. Maybe later, when you feel better, we can talk. Right now I want you to rest. I'll bring in something to eat as soon as I get it fixed."

Jesse's eyes drifted shut before she'd closed the door on her way out. He slept the sleep of exhaustion and sickness, with only vague memories of reviving enough to swallow a few bites of some delicious soup the woman fed him. When he roused later in the morning, a little girl sat beside his bed, a rag doll on her lap.

"Hello." The one word caused Jesse to cough, although this time wasn't as severe as earlier. She stood next to the bed and patted his cheek until he could relax. The well-worn doll hung limply over her other arm, its skinny arms and legs dangling in the air.

"Meggie said you aren't to talk, but I have to watch you." The girl held one finger up as if lecturing a recalcitrant child. "Since you can't say anything, I'll tell you all about us so you won't be bored." Jesse nodded. The girl perched on the edge of the chair, a prim little miss replacing the mischievous pixie he'd seen before.

"My name is Seana, and you're at our house." She arranged the doll on her lap. "My sister, Meggie, is outside feeding the animals. She says I can't go outside because it's too cold and the snow is too deep. I just got over being sick, too. She brought your horse in the house. He dripped water everywhere on the floor and made the house stink." Her freckled nose wrinkled. "I don't want you to be mad at Meggie. She had to look in your saddlebags. We needed to know your name. She said Papa would have done that, too."

Sadness clouded Seana's eyes. "Papa and Momma and Matt went to town. They still aren't home. Meggie says they probably stayed with the Porters. Reverend Porter talks a lot in church on Sundays. We don't get to hear him very often because Yankton is too far away." She leaned forward and lowered her voice to a whisper. "I'm glad because I never understand the words he says. He makes me want to sleep."

Jesse's lips twitched. He'd met a few ministers who put him to sleep, too. The one at his parents' church, for instance. That man spoke in such a pompous monotone that Jesse wondered if even God stayed awake to listen.

"This is my doll, Ennis. I named her after my grandmother." The doll's features were worn, with several of the stitches of her mouth missing. The matted yarn that made up her hair hung in various lengths. Her button eyes still shone, but Seana would have to be careful or the few threads holding them would come loose.

"My momma made this dress for her at Christmas. She made me a dress just like Ennis's, but I can only wear mine for church or weddings." She frowned. "We don't have many weddings, either, so I've only worn the dress when we went to church at Christmastime."

A gust of cold air rushed into the room. The sound of a door closing heralded the arrival of Megan from outside. Jesse opened his mouth to say something, but Seana leaped to her feet and held up that warning finger again.

"Don't you talk or Meggie will get mad at me." She looked so serious, Jesse wanted to hug her and laugh at the same time.

"Seana, have you been bothering Mr. Coulter?" Megan appeared in the doorway, her cheeks and nose bright red from the cold. "I told you he needed to rest."

"He woke up. He tried to talk and I told him not to. I've been telling him all about Momma and Papa. He even met Ennis." Seana held up her doll as if presenting evidence of doing right.

Megan's lips twitched. "You did just fine, Seana." She turned to Jesse, her eyes downcast. "Get some rest, Mr. Coulter. I'll fix you something to eat. You have to build up your strength." She began to back out of the door. "Come along, Seana. Let Mr. Coulter sleep while you help me."

Jesse closed his eyes. From the floating feeling washing through his body, he knew full recovery might take some time. As tired as he was, he couldn't seem to relax. A jumble of thoughts tumbled through his brain. The picture of Meggie and her refusal to look at him, as if she were ashamed of something. The question of where God wanted him to go to preach. He wanted to go the right direction, but didn't have a clear idea which way that would be. He sighed, drifting toward sleep. Due to this sickness, he would have plenty of time to seek out God's direction. Perhaps He wanted Jesse to continue his trek to the Dakota gold fields and begin preaching there.

❧

That night Megan couldn't sleep. Visions of her parents caught in the blizzard wouldn't leave. Although she'd assured Seana their parents and Matt probably stayed in Yankton, she wasn't sure. Her mother had been very worried about Seana's fever. She promised to make Papa leave early so they could be back before dark, if possible. The trip took half a day; but if they hurried with the shopping, they could have been back on the road shortly after lunchtime.

The storm had come in the afternoon. Heavy clouds in the sky had given some indication of bad weather, but no one could have guessed the fast drop in temperature or the severity of the blizzard. Megan hadn't been sure she would have time to put up guide ropes because the snow hit so hard and furious. If her family had already begun the trip home, they may have been trapped in the open. Tears burned her eyes at the thought. Every day that passed made her think something was wrong.

This afternoon, while Seana and Mr. Coulter were both asleep, Megan had gone outside. In the bright sunlight, the white snow hurt her eyes. She'd gone to the barn and climbed up on a fence, trying to get as high as possible to see if her parents' wagon was in sight. Nothing marred the white expanse in any direction. She'd watched until her toes and fingers went numb, praying for a sign of life somewhere, to no avail.

What if something had happened to them? She didn't want to face that possibility, but inside she knew she might have to. What would happen to her and Seana? She didn't want to leave this country and go back east. They didn't have any close family there who would care for them. As harsh as this land could be, Megan didn't want to leave. She loved this place.

Please, God, let Momma and Papa come home tomorrow. Help them to be safe. Megan turned her face into the pillow and wept silent tears. She drifted off to sleep praying tomorrow would bring good news. The seed of an idea gave her hope. Mr. Coulter and Seana were both stronger. Perhaps she could take Mr. Coulter's horse and go looking for her missing family. On horseback, the trip to town wouldn't take nearly as long. Maybe right after lunch she could go while they rested.

The morning dawned bright and clear. The blue sky made a sharp contrast with the whitened ground. A few clouds scudded past, but nothing looked like more storms. Megan hurried with the feeding and once more climbed the fence, balancing precariously as she looked around. Nothing moved as far as she could see. She climbed back down, gathered a sled full of wood, and returned to the house. Pasting a smile on her face, she did her best to act as if nothing was wrong so she wouldn't worry Seana.

"Good morning." Megan's hands shook as she carried the bowl of porridge to Mr. Coulter. She couldn't meet his eyes. During his sickness, she spent hours praying for him and watching him. She'd never met a man so handsome and fascinating. She almost wished he were sick again so she could wipe his brow and watch again the play of emotions crossing his face as he slept and dreamed.

"Morning." The word came out a scratchy whisper. He cleared his throat and tried again. "Good morning."

Megan set the tray on the table in the room. "Would you like me to help you sit up some? It might make eating a little easier."

"Thank you." He eased up, and she plumped an extra pillow behind his back to prop him up. She'd never been so close to such an attractive man. Her heart pounded like it did when Matt used to chase her across the fields.

"Would you like me to feed you, Mr. Coulter?"

"Jesse."

Startled, she glanced up. His twinkling brown gaze held her captive for a moment. She looked down at the tray in her hands, her cheeks hot with embarrassment. "What?"

"My name is Jesse. Mr. Coulter sounds so formal." He started to cough, although the sound wasn't quite as alarming as it had been yesterday. By the time he stopped, his face had paled and he seemed tired.

"I'll feed myself. Thank you."

Placing the tray on his lap, Megan stepped back. "If you need anything else. . . Well, I guess you won't be able to call me. I'll come in to check on you or send Seana. She's almost done with her breakfast." She hurried from the room before she wore the man out with her chatter. Not in years had she said so much to a man. What had come over her?

"Mr. Coulter, would you like some more coffee?"

Megan stilled, listening for the answer to her sister's question. A low rumble told her he'd said something, but she couldn't make out the words.

"Meggie would be mad if I did that. Momma says I always have to call adults by their proper name." Seana lowered her voice to a loud whisper. Megan knew Seana didn't think she would hear. "I think Jesse is a wonderful name, though."

Soft, deep laughter sent a shaft of warmth through Megan. Although she didn't wish Mr. Coulter the inconvenience of being injured and sick, she was glad the Lord led him here. Seana needed the distraction of caring for him so she wouldn't worry about her parents and brother. In fact, she admitted, the diversion helped her, too.

The morning sped past. Megan could feel a knot of worry in her stomach. She needed to ask Mr. Coulter—Jesse—if she could use his horse this afternoon, but the thought of approaching the man with such a request terrified her. What if he said no? Would she have the courage to go against his wishes? The building concern for her family told her she must do something.

A knock sounded on the door as Megan popped some biscuits into the oven for their lunch. She'd just been building her courage to approach Mr. Coulter and stared at the door as if she hadn't heard the sound right. Seana skipped out of her parents' bedroom, where she'd been regaling their patient with a myriad of stories.

"Meggie, we have company. Maybe it's Momma and Papa." She ran to open the door, her braids bouncing. Dread crept up Megan's spine, knowing her parents would never knock on the door. They would just come in.

Cold air whooshed into the house as Seana threw open the door. Two people, bundled against the cold, stood waiting.

"Mrs. Porter, Reverend, please come in." Megan's heart pounded loud enough to be heard in town. Her knees wobbled. The Porters came in, stomping the snow from their boots. Megan stared at them as Seana backed toward her, eyes wide, her doll clutched tight to her breast.

"Please, sit down." Megan's voice shook. "Let me get you some coffee. You've had a long ride in the cold." Her hands trembled as she retrieved some cups from the shelves. Fear clutched at her throat with hard fingers. Tears pushed at the back of her eyes.

"Megan, Dear, sit down." Mrs. Porter took the cups from Megan and guided her to a chair. With one arm, she drew Seana to her side, while her other hand rested on Megan's shoulder.

Reverend Porter cleared his throat. "There isn't any easy way to say this. This was a mighty bad storm, the worst I ever recall. The sheriff found your parents and brother late yesterday." He lifted his chin and twisted his neck as if his collar had tightened. "Your family started home before the storm. We think they tried to make it back to town and got off the road in the heavy snow. I'm sorry, but they froze to death."

The world turned dark. Megan couldn't get her breath. She heard Seana scream something, and then her sister was crying, her thin arms wrapped around Megan's neck. Mrs. Porter made clucking noises as if that would help them with their loss. All Megan could think was that her fears had come true, and God hadn't answered her prayers. What would they do now?

As if sensing her uncertainty, Reverend Porter cleared his throat. "I know this is a difficult time, but I wanted to let you know as soon as possible. We told the sheriff we'd break the news to you and let you know that we'll be bringing the bodies out here in a few days, after we make some pine boxes." He cleared his throat again. "We figured you'd want to bury them here at your farm."

Megan did her best to stifle her sobs. The tears continued to flow unheeded down her cheeks. Seana still had her face buried in Megan's neck.

five

The next two days were a blur. Megan occupied the time caring for Mr. Coulter. Seana moved about in stunned silence. Reverend and Mrs. Porter showed up again with Augustus Sparks—the banker—and the sheriff. The men carefully unloaded three pine boxes from the back of a wagon and placed them at the back of the barn.

Megan watched them, tight-lipped. *The last indignity. The ground is too frozen for them to be buried.*

When that task was finished, the men entered the house, stomping their snowy boots. Mrs. Porter fussed around, pouring hot coffee, murmuring useless sympathy.

Dully, Megan wondered why they had enlisted the banker to help, but he put a quick end to her speculation. Waving away the cup Mrs. Porter proffered, he stepped toward Megan. His double chin jiggled as he moved. Dark eyes narrowed as he gave Megan a lecherous grin. "Miss Riley, your father had a loan with my bank. The note is due this June. With all that's happened, I don't know how you'll ever be able to pay it off."

Megan felt as if her world dropped away. Knowing that her parents were dead—and that their bodies rested in the barn—was bad enough. Having this repulsive man tell her more bad news was too much.

"Now, Megan, Mr. Sparks does have a solution to your dilemma." Reverend Porter spoke in the same sonorous tones he used in church. "Mr. Sparks has generously agreed to marry you and take care of the note himself."

Mr. Sparks's grin widened.

Megan felt reality swirling away. "I. . .I can't marry you."

Her tongue felt like a huge cotton boll. "I won't." The tremor in her voice lacked the conviction she was hoping to convey.

"Now, Dear." Mrs. Porter patted her shoulder. "I know this has all been a nasty shock, but you can't possibly expect us to leave you in such terrible straits. Mr. Sparks is making a very generous offer. He's willing to take on a new wife. He'll care for your sister, too."

The banker peeled the gloves off his sausagelike fingers and began to unbutton his coat. "I don't believe you have any other choice, young lady. You can't stay out here in the middle of nowhere with no man around to care for you. I'm sure you and your sister will enjoy the amenities that come from living in town."

"He's right." Reverend Porter gestured for his wife to serve the coffee, as though this were his own house and Megan's situation would be readily solved. "Yankton has a lot of young ladies your age. Your sister will be able to attend school. Augustus here has just about the best house in town. Now we can perform the ceremony here, or we can wait until we get back to town. Which will it be?"

Megan could feel all of their gazes boring into her. She couldn't seem to get her breath. How could they expect something like this to happen right now? Even her parents hadn't cared for the banker. They only dealt with him out of necessity. They would never approve of such a union.

Giving Seana a squeeze, she urged her to stand. "Seana, please go to your room for a little while. I'll be along shortly."

Seana opened her mouth as if she wanted to argue. Glancing around at the others in the room, she nodded and scuffed her feet as she left. With her sister out of sight, Megan stood and faced the men. Locking her knees, she hoped they wouldn't see the tremors quaking through her. She'd been taught never to speak up to adults; but if they were considering marrying her off like some animal going to the highest bidder, she would have her say first.

"I don't know how you can expect me to do this. I've barely learned my parents and brother are dead, and you immediately want me to get married as if I can forget something that important. What about a period of mourning? Mr. Sparks, I'm sure you intend this as a kind offer, but I will not marry you now or ever. My sister and I will stay here on the farm and care for the land. I've helped my parents for years now."

"But my dear, how can you possibly plant the fields?" Mrs. Porter handed coffee to the men and turned to face Megan. "You won't be able to support yourself."

"And there's the loan to pay off. June is only six months away." Mr. Sparks spoke as if he were already rubbing his hands together.

"We will manage." Megan spoke more firmly than she felt. "Our hogs have done well this year. We have several young ones. Yankton already knows that my mother and I make the best sausages and hams." Her voice cracked at the mention of her mother. "Seana and I can make things and bring them to town to sell them. Perhaps since Mr. Sparks is in such a generous mood, he'll be willing to extend our loan. After all, these are unusual circumstances." She didn't add that she wouldn't be able to make any more meat to sell until next fall, when the young piglets would be big enough. Her father had already done the butchering for this winter.

"I'm afraid that will be impossible." Mr. Sparks attempted a forlorn look, but his gaze still made Megan want to turn and run.

"What happens if some unsavory character comes along?" The sheriff leaned forward. "You won't have anyone out here to protect you. This is a mighty far piece from town."

"My father taught me how to shoot a gun, Sheriff. I'm perfectly capable of protecting my sister and myself." Megan wanted to stamp her foot. "I will not marry Mr. Sparks no matter how kind his offer is. You will have to accept that."

"My dear." Mrs. Porter patted her shoulder again, causing Megan to grit her teeth at the woman's conciliatory tone. "There's been talk in town. We know about what happened to you back East. I'm sure you've noticed none of the young men have come to call on you. With your past, Mr. Sparks is perhaps your only chance at marriage."

"That's true." The reverend frowned, his disapproving tone echoing off the walls. "I believe you have no choice here. The sheriff and Mr. Sparks had the foresight to have the wedding right here and now. This will save you some embarrassment. I know there'll be talk because of your reputation and all; but as people become used to you, they'll forget."

"I want you to leave now." Megan spoke through clenched teeth. "I have nothing in my past to be ashamed of, other than the lies people spread about me." She began to shake. "You can take your *generous* offer of marriage and get out of here and leave my sister and me to our grief."

"I'm afraid we can't do that." Reverend Porter extracted a book from a deep coat pocket. "My wife and I consider this our Christian duty to see that you're taken care of properly. Now, if you will join Mr. Sparks here. The sheriff and my wife can be the witnesses."

They weren't listening. Megan couldn't believe this was happening. She was going to end up married to this repulsive man, and no one would hear what she was trying to say. Frantic thoughts tumbled through her mind. What would her mother do? Her father? She knew how the Porters learned of the travesty that happened to her before they moved here, but what about the others in town?

The four adults moved to surround Megan. She could smell the wet cloth from the outdoor clothing they still wore. She understood their hurry if they wanted to get back to town before nightfall. The air grew close. She wished she could faint or do something drastic to delay the inevitable. Reverend Porter opened his book and cleared his throat.

"I believe the lady said she didn't want to get married."

Everyone's gaze swung to the door of her parents' bedroom. Jesse leaned against the frame, a quilt wrapped around his broad shoulders, his bare feet protruding beneath. Megan's face flamed as she realized how this would look to these townsfolk. Their eyes widened, and she knew they weren't seeing Mr. Coulter as someone recovering from a sickness, but as a drifter taking advantage of a young woman. Even his face, covered with several days' growth of stubble, gave him a lawless look—one she found very appealing, although she had no right to think such thoughts.

"What is going on here?" Reverend Porter's face had turned beet red. "Who is this man?"

Megan opened her mouth to answer, but nothing came out. She knew the truth wouldn't be believable. Hadn't she told the truth before they moved here and none of the townspeople believed her? Even her parents didn't seem to understand the wrong done to her.

"Jesse Coulter." Jesse nodded his head, but didn't offer to cross the room to shake hands. Megan almost groaned. She knew he didn't have the strength to walk across the room, but none of the others knew that. They would assume he was being insolent, as many drifters were.

The reverend's hard gaze bore into Megan. "I didn't want to believe what we'd been told. I know how gossip can hurt a person, but this is proof that your reputation has been sullied. Did you have this man waiting and rush him in as soon as your parents left for town?" His words hit Megan like a gale, almost knocking her from her feet.

❧

Jesse leaned against the door frame and watched Megan's face turn white. His angel. How could they do this to her?

What had she ever done? In the few days he'd been under her care, he'd never met such a thoughtful, hardworking, God-fearing woman before. She defined godly compassion, yet these people were accusing her of being a horrible person. He couldn't allow that.

When he'd first heard the conversation through the partially opened bedroom door, he grieved with her when he learned of the death of her family. She hadn't said a word about it to him the last two days, though he'd been too sick with the fever to have known, anyway. But disbelief pushed away the hurt as he listened to Megan being railroaded into marrying some man she didn't want. He knew he had to do something to help her out. His clothes weren't available, so he covered himself with the quilt, thinking he would be presentable enough. He hadn't thought about how this would look. He only wanted to protect Megan. Now he'd made things worse.

He tried to make his muscles move. Before getting sick, he could have thrown these men from the house with no trouble. Because of the pneumonia, he'd barely made it to the doorway. He hadn't even said anything for a minute because he couldn't get his breath, and the room was spinning so bad he thought he might faint, throw up, or both.

"This is not what you're thinking." Megan's fingers were twined together tight enough to look painful. "Mr. Coulter is sick."

"I don't want to hear any of your excuses." Reverend Porter's brows drew together, giving him the look of a storm cloud about to burst.

The overweight banker stared at Jesse with a venomous gaze. The sheriff unbuttoned his greatcoat to reveal a holstered pistol strapped to his side. His huge mustache accentuated his frown. Mrs. Porter stood frozen beside Megan, her hand covering her mouth, looking as if she wanted to cry.

"Reverend, I would think you should recall Matthew 7:1."

Jesse stood his ground as the angry minister glared at him. " 'Judge not, that ye be not judged.' " Silence stretched taut in the room.

"I'd like to know who you are and where you came from." The sheriff strode over to confront Jesse.

"My name is Jesse Coulter. I'm from outside the Chicago area. I was passing through on my way to the gold mines in the Black Hills when I got caught in the blizzard." He looked past the sheriff to where Megan stood pale, but strong. "If it hadn't been for the young lady you're accusing, I'd have been dead. She saved my life."

"The blizzard ended days ago. Why are you still here?" The sheriff leaned forward. "I agree with the reverend. This doesn't look very proper."

"I caught pneumonia." Jesse shrugged. "I've been too sick to leave." Weakness pulled at him. He longed to crawl back to that bed and sleep for a week. How much longer could he stand here before he fell flat?

"He's right. This is the first time he's been able to get up since he's been here."

Megan took a step toward him, but Mrs. Porter caught her arm, pulling her back. "You mean you took care of this man for several days? You're not married."

Megan whirled on the minister's wife. "Mrs. Porter, the man was dying. What would Jesus do in such circumstances? Leave him to freeze to death? Let him die of pneumonia?"

"This just wasn't proper." Mrs. Porter glanced at her husband. "What will the townspeople think? After all, they've all heard the rumors of that incident with the young man where you used to live."

"And just how did they *all* hear that?" Megan took a step closer. Jesse bit back a smile at the thought that Megan might throw these people out without any help from him. "Did you make sure they knew all about what happened? I know my parents talked to you and your husband. They trusted you not to spread that information all over." The chill in the room rivaled the freezing temperatures outside.

Mrs. Porter's face reddened. "I. . .I don't know how the townspeople learned of your misfortune. Perhaps your parents told others."

"They wouldn't have told anyone else." Megan took another step closer, her fists clenched at her sides. "The only reason they talked to you was because they believed in being open with their pastor. Our whole family was hurt by those false accusations, and they needed to talk to you."

Megan turned away, and Jesse could see the tears in her eyes. She half-turned to face Mrs. Porter. Jesse strained to hear what she said. "You betrayed my parents' trust. I think that's worse than anything you're accusing me of doing."

"That's enough." Reverend Porter towered over Megan. He yanked on his black coat and glared at her. "I won't have you maligning my wife. You're the one in the wrong here."

He faced the banker. "Mr. Sparks, I'm sorry, but I don't believe you'll be wanting to marry this young lady now."

The banker stuttered. Yanking a handkerchief from his pocket, he wiped his face, even though the room was chilly. "I realize the circumstances have changed somewhat, but I'm still willing to be wed. It's obvious to me this young lady needs a strong man to care for her and keep her in line."

Jesse couldn't see the look the banker gave Megan, but her reaction made his insides tighten. He longed to be able to help her. He wanted to force these people out of the house, but his body wouldn't respond to any of the commands he tried to give. Even his brain felt fuzzy from exhaustion. Something had to happen soon or he would end up in a heap on the floor.

"I will not marry you." Megan glared at the banker, and Jesse wanted to cheer for her.

"I'm astonished at Mr. Sparks's generosity toward you,

Megan." The reverend's smile for the banker changed to a scowl as he faced Megan. "I refuse to leave here today without seeing you become a respectable woman. It's obvious to my wife and me that you need someone to care for you. Mr. Sparks is a good match. I'm appalled at your lack of enthusiasm over his offer." He stepped closer, his tone becoming threatening. "Would you rather marry that poor excuse for a man who's standing half-naked over there? Is a penniless drifter better than a respected man like Mr. Sparks?"

Hands on her hips, Megan matched him glare for glare. "I would rather marry anyone than Mr. Sparks. I don't consider this a generous offer. He only wants to get his grubby hands on my father's land, just as he's done with countless others around here. He makes generous loans and then forecloses on the land without any consideration for who lives there. My parents would never approve of a marriage between Mr. Sparks and me. Now, will you kindly leave my home?" She flung her arm in a gesture toward the door.

"You have no choice about the matter, Megan. With your parents dead and you alone, the sheriff and I have taken it on ourselves to look after you. Mr. Sparks says you won't be able to pay off the loan. We can't have you thrown off your land. You have your sister to think about, too. She'll need caring for."

"He's right, Dear." Mrs. Porter tried to pat Megan's shoulder, but Megan jerked out of her reach. "I don't know where you got those horrible ideas about Mr. Sparks. He's a fine, upstanding citizen. He'll take good care of you."

Reverend Porter opened his black book again and cleared his throat. The sheriff moved to stand beside the banker. Mrs. Porter took a firm grip on Megan's arm. Jesse could see the look of panic that crossed Megan's face. His angel. He couldn't allow this to happen to her.

"I'll marry her." Before he could glance around to see who had spoken, Jesse realized the words had come from his mouth.

six

"I believe that's highly inappropriate." Reverend Porter spoke first. "Since we are in charge of this young lady's welfare, my dear wife and I would never see her married to a common drifter."

"I am not a common drifter." Jesse tried to stand taller.

"And just who would you be?" The sheriff took one threatening step forward.

"My father, Richard Coulter, is the owner of the First Central Bank of Chicago." He gave a tight smile. "So you see, Megan would be changing from one banker to another."

"You said you were going to the gold mines." Sheriff Armstrong narrowed his eyes.

"I have recently taken a leave of absence from the bank. I wanted to do a bit of traveling." Jesse swallowed hard against the half-lie. He had wanted to travel, but he hadn't intended to ever return to the bank or to the Chicago area. He couldn't look at Megan, fearing to see a look of disappointment in her eyes. Most likely she didn't want to marry him, either, but he could see no other way to keep her from being tied to a man she despised.

"This is preposterous." Mr. Sparks huffed. "We have no proof that he is who he says. This man could be anyone posing as a banker."

"He's telling the truth." Megan's soft whisper caused a hush to fall.

"How do you know that, Child?" Reverend Porter asked.

"When he was so sick, I looked through his things." She hesitated, glancing at Jesse and then away. "I wanted to see

44

who to inform if he didn't live. He was so sick." She squared her shoulders. "He had some papers in his bag from the First Central Bank. I didn't read through them closely, but I did see the name of Richard Coulter on the papers."

"He could be making this up." Mr. Sparks wiped at his face with his handkerchief.

"No, he had a Bible in his belongings. That's how Seana and I knew his name."

"Meggie?" Seana peeked around the curtain. Megan held out her arms, and her sister dashed across the room and flung herself at Megan. "Meggie, please don't marry Mr. Sparks. You know what Papa said about him." Seana gave Mr. Sparks a pointed look as she tried to whisper, but everyone could hear what she said.

"I won't marry him, Seana."

"You will have to be wed, Megan." Reverend Porter frowned at her. "Your virtue has been brought into question. We can't have your reputation sullied further than it is." He glanced at his wife. "However, I will give you the choice of which banker you will marry."

Megan's eyes sparkled with unshed tears. Jesse ached for her. How could these people be so thoughtless? To be forced to make such a decision, when her family wasn't even buried, was cruel. "Perhaps you would give the young lady a few days to consider the choice before she makes it."

"That would never work." Mrs. Porter looked horrified. "Megan either has to marry you in order to stay here tonight, or she has to marry Mr. Sparks and leave with us. Knowing that you are here virtually unchaperoned leaves us no other choice, isn't that right, Dear?"

Reverend Porter nodded. "Megan, you must choose now or we will make the decision for you. We have to get back to town before too much time passes."

"I will never marry Mr. Sparks." Megan repeated the words

with such force that Jesse had no doubts, but he wondered why she didn't say she would rather marry him. Didn't she like him, either? Confusion swirled through his mind. He couldn't seem to focus on anything any longer. His legs turned soft, and he slid down to sit on the floor with a thump. He tried to force a smile when they all turned to look at him, but none of his muscles seemed to be in working order.

&

"Jesse." Megan's heart thudded as she watched him slump to the floor. He'd been so sick. He shouldn't have been out of bed at all, let alone for this long. Eternity seemed to have passed as they stood here debating her future, as if she had no significance. Megan hurried across the room and knelt beside Jesse. Her fingers touched his brow to find him slightly warmer than he should have been. She hoped his fever wasn't returning.

"What's the matter with him?" Sheriff Armstrong knelt beside her.

"I told you he's been sick. He's had pneumonia from the exposure he suffered during the blizzard. He shouldn't even be up and about. Help me get him back to bed." Megan tried to get her shoulder underneath his arm. Jesse tried to stand, but he didn't appear to have any strength left.

"Here, let me help with that." Reverend Porter pushed her aside. Between them, he and the sheriff managed to get Jesse back to bed. Megan tucked the covers around him and wiped the sweat from his brow with a damp cloth.

"Now, you see, we can't possibly go through with this. This man is as sick as I told you."

"It's still improper for you to be here with him." Reverend Porter's chin jutted out. "We'll give him a few minutes to recover. When he's awake enough to repeat his vows, we'll get you married."

"She should marry me." Mr. Sparks's face reddened. "I offered to be her husband. It was a generous offer, considering her background. I won't see her wed to some stranger we don't even know."

"Sometimes God makes other choices for us." Reverend Porter gestured at the man on the bed. "If you were to marry her, you would always have this hanging over your head. People would talk about how she spent these days with a stranger in her house. Having her wed him is the best way, especially since we know he's a man of means."

A slight smile appeared on Jesse's face. Megan watched him open his eyes, although he didn't seem to focus. She couldn't help but wonder what little joke ran through his mind at the reverend's words. Had he lied about who he was? Her emotions swinging with the wind, Megan didn't know what to think anymore. All she wanted was to curl up in a corner and grieve for her parents and Matt, to hold Seana and not think about the future.

Hours later, only the glow of the fire lit the main room of the house. Flickering images danced across the walls, but Megan paid them little attention. Huddled in an old quilt her mother stitched for her years ago, she allowed the tears to flow unchecked. Pain, hard physical pain, flared through her chest as she thought of her mother, father, and brother, their frozen bodies waiting in the barn until the ground thawed enough to dig the graves.

Dear God, what are we supposed to do now? How will I ever manage without Momma? Fresh tears traced down her cheeks. She could clearly recall the morning her parents left for town, although it seemed a lifetime ago now. The smell of cooking breakfast, ham and coffee, clung to her mother as she hugged Megan. Her father kissed her cheek, the touch of his beard tickling against her skin as he bid her good-bye. Matt with his saucy grin, hopping into the bed of the wagon in one easy jump. She could see how the legs of his pants were too short already, knowing her mother had left a big hem for this reason. Matt sprouted up faster than they could keep him in clothes. Never again would she hug them or talk to them.

"Momma, I'm married now," Megan whispered the words aloud. "I'm not sure Jesse even knows or understands that we're married. He did say the words, but his fever was up and his eyes didn't quite focus." Megan closed her eyes and fought a wave of anguish at the travesty of being married on the same day her family's bodies were brought home.

If Seana hadn't been there to see Reverend Porter perform the ceremony, Megan would be tempted to tell Jesse he'd had a dream. He'd been so sick, he would probably believe her. He would leave when he got well, and no one would bother her again. The townsfolk would still believe her married.

"What am I to do about the loan, Papa? How did you plan to pay it off?" She shuddered at the thought of the greedy look in Mr. Sparks's eyes. The man wanted all he could get. He saw the possibilities for this area to grow, and he wanted to own as much of it as possible. He wasn't beyond doing anything to anyone to get his way. Her father had returned home one afternoon, grim and withdrawn after assisting a neighbor who'd been evicted by Mr. Sparks. The banker stood by with a smile on his face the whole time the family made haste to pack.

"Where will we go if we can't pay the loan? He'll throw us out the same as he did the Sheffields, especially after I treated him so poorly today." Megan pressed her fingers to her burning eyes. She couldn't let this get her down. Her parents always insisted that God was in charge and He could be trusted, but Megan was beginning to wonder. Their trust in God left them frozen to death in a blizzard, with the possibility of eminent foreclosure on their property.

God, I don't know how You could do this to people who loved You as much as Momma and Papa did. If You're in charge, why did You leave Seana and me without any family?

Why did You allow me to marry a man I don't even know and who probably has no desire to be married to me?

No answers came, but then Megan hadn't expected any.

৯

The smell of frying bacon tickled Jesse's nose. His stomach growled. He stretched, reveling in the warmth of the bed contrasted to the cold of the room he slept in. Drawing in a breath, he tested his lungs to see how much air he could pull in without coughing. When he felt the catch in his chest, he froze, then slowly breathed out.

His body didn't feel as sluggish this morning, and he wondered if he could get out of bed. He hadn't been up since this sickness weakened him. He frowned. Of course, there was that crazy dream he had last night. Shaking his head, he chuckled. Imagine him getting married. That had to be an illusion. He'd just promised God he would go wherever the Lord led, so he knew getting married and settling down wasn't for him. He might live his whole life without a wife. His thoughts strayed to Megan. Of course, if he had to become a husband to someone, she would be a good choice. He would always carry a fondness for his angel.

The bedroom door edged open, and Seana's face peeked around. At the sight of him awake, she lit up like a summer day. "Meggie, he's awake." She flung the door the rest of the way open and bounded into the room, her braids bouncing across her shoulders.

Sliding to a stop, Seana leaned her elbows on the bed and gave Jesse a peculiar smile. He couldn't begin to guess what was going on behind those sparkling blue eyes. "Megan sent me to see if you were awake and if you wanted some real food for breakfast. She's cooking bacon and eggs. I have to slice some bread, too, and there's coffee."

Jesse chuckled. When had he last felt such enthusiasm? No wonder Jesus mentioned coming to Him as a child. Who wouldn't be drawn to one like Seana? A loud rumble inter-rupted his thoughts. Seana covered her mouth with her hand and giggled.

"I guess that's your answer. The smell of that bacon woke me up. I can almost taste it from here."

"I'll tell Meggie." With that, Seana bounded across the room and disappeared from sight.

A few minutes later, Megan came in carrying a tray laden with his breakfast. She appeared more shy than usual, her gaze downcast, a hesitancy about her that hadn't been there before. Had he done something to offend her? Thinking hard, Jesse couldn't recall anything he'd said or done. He bit back a grin. Thank goodness, she wasn't privilege to his dreams. If she knew he'd dreamed about them having a wedding, she'd be running rather than bringing him food.

"Good morning."

Megan flinched at his words, sloshing coffee from the cup onto the tray. A flush spread over her round cheeks, giving her a rosy fresh appeal. Jesse wanted to do something to make her smile so he could see the dimple in her cheek. He picked up the fork instead, wondering why he would be thinking of such things when he would be leaving this place soon and never see these people again.

"Good morning, Mr. Coulter. Are you feeling better this morning?" Megan spoke so softly, he had to strain to catch the words even though she stood beside him. Her tone held a touch of something different. Fear? Uncertainty?

"I'm feeling much stronger, thank you. I believe I'll try to get up as soon as I eat." He scooped up a bite of eggs. "It will be good to finally get out of bed. I'll see if I can remember how to walk. Maybe by tomorrow I can get out of your way."

Megan paled. She stepped back. "I'll be back to get your tray." She rushed from the room. Jesse stared after her, won-dering what could possibly be wrong. Up until now Megan had been sweet and caring. He'd enjoyed the way she sat with him, talking on occasion, but mostly watching over him. After breakfast he would have to find out about the sudden change in behavior.

Feeling stronger after eating, Jesse asked for some water to wash with and his clothes. Megan brought both, then retreated in uncharacteristic silence. This time he noted the dark circles under her red-rimmed eyes. Why had she been crying?

Seana waited outside when he opened the door. Standing up took more energy than he thought it would. Just getting washed and dressed drained him so much, he wasn't sure he could make the trek across the room to a chair. Sweat beaded on his forehead. Seana frowned at him as he rested one hand on the door frame.

"Meggie, I think he's gonna fall like he did yesterday."

Yesterday? When had he fallen yesterday? He hadn't been out of bed until now. Before he could question Seana's statement, Megan was beside him, helping him to a chair. He'd never felt so stupid as he did now having a woman assist him in walking. Jesse hated this sickness. He sank into the rocker with a grateful sigh.

"I'm not sure you should be up and about yet, Mr. Coulter." Megan wiped his brow.

"Why not, Meggie?" Seana patted him on the arm. "He got up yesterday right before he married you."

seven

Lifting another shovel of manure from the stall floor, Jesse tried his best to ignore the pine boxes in the back of the barn. In the past few weeks, since he'd learned he was married to Megan, he'd done his best to take over the chores and save her the heartache of seeing these reminders of her family.

Married! He thrust the shovel into the muck covering the floor. He'd made a promise to God, and now he couldn't keep it. When he recovered, he'd planned to leave and follow wherever the Lord led him, just like Jonah went to Nineveh. Under Pastor Phillips's tutelage, he'd learned a lot about the Bible. He could preach a sermon with the best of them and had, on occasion, assisted the pastor. This was God's call for his life. He'd been running from that call, yet now he wasn't running; he was at a dead stop.

Taking a handkerchief from his pocket, Jesse wiped the sweat from his face. He leaned against the post by the stall door and surrendered to the fatigue washing through him. This job should have taken him half an hour to do, but the lack of energy that plagued him made every chore stretch out three or four times longer than it should. Megan assured him her brother, Matt, had the same problem after he had pneumonia. Still, he felt like a useless old man most of the time.

The door creaked, then crashed against the side of the barn as a gust of wind caught it. Seana stumbled inside, her pale cheeks rosy from the cold, her doll, Ennis, clutched to her chest. Jesse hurried to grab the door and shut out the fierce wind.

"Seana, what are you doing? Does Megan know you're outside?"

Hugging her arms tight around her frail body, Seana shook her head. Jesse could see the snow clumped over the top of her boots. Her feet would be frozen if he didn't get her back in the house soon. He reached for her, but she backed away.

"Don't touch me." She held out her hand in front of her as if that would keep him away. "Megan won't let me come to see Momma and Papa, but I have to." Tears glittered in her eyes. Jesse could see all the hurt and anger she'd been holding back brimming to the surface.

He held out his hand. "I'll take you to them."

She sniffed. He could see she wanted to refuse. Sniffing again, Seana let him take her small hand in his. He led her to the back of the barn. A small barrel rested across from the boxes. Jesse knew about the times Megan sneaked out here after Seana went to sleep. He'd kept her secret so far, but he always watched the time, unwilling to let her stay too long in the frigid weather.

Easing down on the barrel, Jesse lifted Seana onto his lap. He snuggled her close, hoping to give her some of his warmth. A calico cat meowed and wound around his legs. Seana bent down to pet her.

"This is Mama Kitty. That's Shadow." She pointed to the gray cat hiding behind a pile of hay. "They help us keep the mice away from the feed." Seana leaned back against Jesse, her gaze on the pine boxes a few feet away.

"Why are they in boxes?" The small sound of Seana's voice made his heart ache.

"Remember what Megan told you about not being able to bury them until the ground thaws? Well, this is a way of keeping them safe until then. And even after they're buried." He rubbed her arm, tucking her head under his chin. "You know, Seana, your parents and Matt aren't in those bodies anymore.

They've gone to live with Jesus now."

"In heaven?"

"Yep. Do you know what heaven is like?"

"There are angels there."

"That's true." Jesse took off his mittens and worked them over her hands and up her arms as far as they would go, careful not to make her drop Ennis. "The Bible talks about heaven being a wonderful place. No one gets sick there or hurt. They don't even have anything to cry about."

"They got hurt here." A small sob shook Seana. "Jesus didn't keep them from dying."

Jesse rocked Seana as she cried. He'd been worried about her lack of emotion over these deaths. She'd laughed and gone on like nothing had happened. He knew it wouldn't last, and now looked like the time for her to grieve. *Jesus, give me the words to help her.*

"You know all the times your parents have gone to town shopping and left you with Megan?" Jesse asked. Seana nodded, her head pressed against his chest. "Did you miss them while they were gone?"

"Yes."

"But you knew they'd be coming home, didn't you?"

"This time they didn't."

"That's true. This time they went to a different home. They went to stay with Jesus." He brushed the hair back from her cheek as she lifted her face to look at him. "But just like they used to come home to you, they're waiting now for you to come home to them."

A lone tear spilled down Seana's cheek. "I can't ever go there. Momma wanted to show me the way, but I didn't want to talk about it."

"Did she tell you the only way to get to heaven is through Jesus, Seana? Did she want you to ask Him to be your Savior?"

She nodded. "Momma talked about that, but I didn't want

to. Now I don't know if I remember how to do it. Maybe Jesus took them away because I was so bad."

"This wasn't to punish you, Seana. Jesus loves you. He loves your whole family. Do you understand what sin is?" Jesse waited as she thought and then nodded her head. "Do you believe Jesus is the Son of God sent to die for our sins?"

"Yes. Momma told me about all that."

"Then all you have to do is ask Him to be your Savior. Jesus is just waiting for you to want Him." Bowing his head, Jesse led Seana in a prayer. This time the ache in his chest wasn't from sickness, but from joy that God had provided such a beautiful answer to his prayer.

"Can I go see them now?" Seana's blue eyes stared up at him.

Jesse gave her a hug and a smile. "Not just yet. You have to wait until it's your time to go to heaven."

"But they'll get lonely for me, won't they?"

"I imagine they look forward to the day you can join them, Seana, but God's time isn't the same as our time. Only a short time will pass for them while you grow up, get married, and have a family of your own. It will be more like a day gone to town to them."

Seana glanced at the bodies and back to him. She gave him a watery smile. "Can I go tell Meggie?"

He hugged her to him. "I think Megan would love to hear, especially about your decision to ask Jesus to be your Savior." Seana hopped off his lap and trotted to the door. Mama Kitty trailed behind her, purring as Seana gave her a final pat before slipping through the door. Jesse followed her, wondering how he'd come to love this little girl in such a short time. Had he also come to love her sister? His wife? Would he ever love her?

❧

Megan grasped behind her to pull the shed door shut as she balanced a basket in her other arm. Her breath blew out in a cloud of white in the chill afternoon air. A weak sun did little to warm anything. Juggling her basket of potatoes and dried vegetables for a stew, she didn't see Seana until her sister leaped forward, wrapping Megan in a fierce hug. Vegetables went flying as the basket dropped to the ground.

"Seana, whatever are you doing outside?" Panic flared through Megan. Her sister's health was always fragile. She couldn't take the extreme cold and had to be protected.

"Meggie, I have something to tell you." Seana's brilliant blue eyes twinkled with excitement.

"Seana, get inside. I'll pick up the vegetables and come in. Then you can tell me what you were doing outside when it's so cold." Megan regretted her harsh tone when some of the sparkle left Seana's eyes.

"Yes, Meggie." Seana let go and began to trudge off to the house, her shoulders slumped.

"Wait." Megan waited until her sister turned back. "Help me pick these up and you can tell me your news while we work."

Seana grinned and bounced back to help Megan. Megan knelt down, grateful that the snow here had packed enough to keep their dinner from disappearing.

"I went to visit Momma, Papa, and Matt."

Megan froze at Seana's words. Anger welled up inside her. How could Seana do that? Hadn't she told her to stay away from the barn? Footsteps crunched in the snow, stopping beside her. She looked up as Seana continued to drop vegetables into the basket. Jesse stood there. For an instant their gazes met and held. Megan knew he understood her thoughts. He knew about the nights she slipped out to sit with her family. As if she could read his thoughts, she saw the hurt she'd done to Seana by not allowing her a time to grieve.

Reaching for a potato, Megan pushed away her roiling emotions. "I'm sorry I didn't take you out there before, Seana. I was so afraid you'd get sick." Her voice caught in her throat.

"I couldn't bear for anything to happen to you, too."

Jesse bent over and picked up the basket. "Looks like you've rescued supper, Ladies. Shall we get inside?"

Megan allowed Jesse to take her hand and help her up. She frowned over his bare hand and opened her mouth to ask why he wasn't wearing any mittens. A glance at Seana gave her the answer. He'd given up his warmth to keep her sister from getting too cold. Gratitude she couldn't express flowed through Megan. In the past few weeks, Jesse had been such a gentleman. He'd worked hard as soon as he could get on his feet. She noticed the lines of fatigue on his face by evening. Not once had he complained about being forced to marry her. He hadn't even said anything about continuing on to the gold fields as she thought he would, and she hadn't had the courage to bring it up.

By the time Megan had the vegetables washed for the stew, Jesse had the fire crackling and the water in the pot. Seana's cheeks and nose were still cherry red when she came out from changing into dry, warmer clothes. Megan frowned, hoping her sister wasn't coming down with another of her fevers so soon. All her childhood had been plagued with sickness. Their mother always said the child caught every little disease that came within a hundred miles.

"I have something else to tell you, Meggie." Seana glanced at Jesse as if she wasn't sure how to continue. He winked at her. "I'm going to live with Momma and Papa."

"You can't possibly stay in the barn, Seana. It's much too cold and dirty."

"Not in the barn. I'm going to heaven." Seana clapped her hands, bouncing on the balls of her feet.

Megan felt as if she'd been kicked by a mule. She could feel the color drain from her face. Her mother had once told her that some people had premonitions of their own deaths. Is this what was happening to Seana? Her fingers gripped the edge of the table before her knees could buckle and send her to the floor.

Strong arms surrounded Megan. Jesse eased her back against his solid form. For once, she welcomed his strength.

"Seana, why don't you tell your sister what we talked about in the barn?"

Seana gave another bounce, oblivious to the turmoil she'd thrown Megan into. "We talked about heaven and how Momma, Papa, and Matt are there. Jesse showed me how to ask Jesus in my heart so I can go there, too." She wrinkled her brow. "He says it may take a long time to me, but to Momma and Papa it will be like a day before I'm there with them."

Tension drained from Megan, leaving her weak-kneed. She sagged back against Jesse, relief pouring through her. He'd known. He understood what she thought and had Seana share her conversion so Megan wouldn't think her sister was going to die soon. How could this man be so perceptive? Her heart warmed. She'd never known anyone like Jesse.

Holding out her arms, Megan waited for Seana to come, then hugged her hard. "This is the best news I could hear. I believe Momma and Papa are rejoicing with the angels." She kissed her sister on the head before releasing her. Flashing Jesse a grateful smile, she busied herself with scraping the vegetables into the pot. If she wasn't careful, this man would become too important to her; and she knew there would come a day when he would leave. There wasn't a man alive who would want to be married to her. With her plump body and plain face, she'd known she would never marry. Jesse had shown his reluctance by his lack of desire to be around her. Every evening as soon as supper was finished, he retired to her parents' room. He never even kissed her like Papa used to kiss Momma. She couldn't blame him. After the disparaging remarks made on their wedding day and the way she looked, he'd have to be stupid to want her.

Quiet had descended on the house by the time Megan finished cleaning up from supper. Seana, tired from her afternoon exploits, hadn't argued at all when Megan sent her to bed. Jesse thanked her for the meal and returned to his room as soon as he finished eating. She mentally forced herself to begin thinking of her parents' room as Jesse's. After all, he was now head of this home. She would have to adjust.

Sinking into the rocking chair, Megan sorted through the mending basket, choosing one of Seana's dresses to work on. After turning up the wick on the lamp, she broke off a piece of thread. The quiet tread of footsteps startled her.

"Seana, what are you doing out of bed?"

A low chuckle greeted her words. "That's the first time I've ever been accused of being a little girl."

Megan's cheeks burned. "I'm sorry, Mr. Coulter. I didn't realize you were still awake."

"Jesse." Jesse scooted a chair close to hers and plopped down, causing the chair to creak in protest. Megan wanted to scold him for not sitting down gently, but held her tongue. "You need to start calling me Jesse. I sound like an old man when you say Mr. Coulter."

Megan knotted her thread, trying to keep her hands from trembling. What did he want? Why was he sitting so close? He'd almost ignored her until now. "Jesse, then." Her voice quivered.

"We need to talk, Megan. I've given you time to grieve for your family. I know it's been hard on you." Jesse leaned forward, his elbows on his knees, his hands almost touching her. "If we're going to save your farm from that banker you dislike so much, then we have to have a plan. I'll need a lot of help from you."

"I don't know what I can do." Megan couldn't seem to concentrate with him so close. "I don't even know how much we owe the bank."

"Then we'll have to take a trip to town as soon as the weather permits and stop in at the bank." Jesse rubbed his hands down his face. "Do you know if your parents had any money set aside to pay toward the loan?"

"They never talked about it. I don't know what Papa planned to do. He never mentioned any loan."

"Well, if we don't figure something out soon, we might just as well pack up and leave here."

Megan gaped at Jesse, forgetting, for the moment, her reluctance to meet his gaze.

eight

Standing at the edge of the open graves, Megan shivered in the raw wind that raced across the land. Tucked against her side, Seana stood silent and forlorn. Megan closed her eyes, trying to focus on the prayer Jesse was saying in remembrance of her parents and Matt, but his words jumbled together in her head, sounds too mixed up to make sense.

She hated the thought that her family would be buried here when they would most likely lose the land in June when the note came due. She and Jesse had scoured the house looking for money her parents might have set back or at least some paperwork on the loan, but they found nothing. In one of Papa's boxes, they found a small amount of cash and a list of seed needed for the spring. He must have planned to use this to purchase the seed for planting, but Jesse concluded there wouldn't be any extra. In one of the flour jars, Megan found her mother's stash of money that she always set aside to buy necessary items such as shoes or material. It wasn't enough, either.

Four weeks ago, they'd gone to town to talk with Mr. Sparks. He'd greeted them cordially enough, giving them the information they needed for the payoff. He refused to show them the original paperwork, saying Lee and Glenna Riley had agreed to the terms; and if Megan and her new husband wanted to keep the farm, they would just have to abide by the amount already listed. After they left, Jesse hadn't said anything all the way home. In fact, he'd been quiet since then.

Megan flinched as the first shovel full of dirt thudded into the grave. She widened her eyes, trying to keep the tears from falling. She'd cried enough in the past two and a half months.

Today would put this difficult time to rest.

"Meggie, I'm c–cold." Seana's teeth chattered in the quiet.

"Take her on inside, Megan. I'll finish up here." Jesse tossed another shovel of dirt, his expression grim.

Wrapping her long coat around Seana to try to warm her, Megan began the slow walk back to the house. The wind pushed at her back like a mischievous child. The ground, freshly thawed, squished underfoot.

A picture of Jesse back there, working to bury her family, filled Megan's thoughts. She'd grown so accustomed to having him here, she couldn't imagine what life would be like when he left; but leave he would. She understood that. There wasn't anything to keep him here. He'd only been biding his time waiting for the spring thaw so he wouldn't have to travel in such miserable weather. She was sure of this, even though he'd never spoken of it. Why would he stay?

Yes, he'd spent hours repairing tools and harnesses, getting everything ready for spring planting. He'd fixed things around the house. When he found out they didn't go to church in the winter because of the distance and the cold, he even prepared Sunday lessons from the Bible so she and Seana wouldn't miss out on the chance to worship. As much as she loved hearing him teach from God's Word, she still didn't believe that God loved her or that anyone could love her. She would never measure up.

The warmth of the house washed over Megan as she removed her wraps. Seana kicked off her boots, then went to stand in front of the fire instead of taking off her coat and scarf.

"Meggie, will I always miss them?" Seana's shoulders slumped.

"I imagine you will. I know I will." Megan knelt in front of her sister and began to unbutton her coat. "We certainly don't want to forget them, do we?" She smiled. "Sometimes we can just talk about the wonderful things we remember about our family. I know they would be happy, and I'm sure Jesse won't mind." She gave Seana a hug, kissing her forehead.

"I'd better fix some hot coffee and get the bread in the oven. When Jesse comes inside, he'll be ready for something to warm him up." Leaving Seana to finish with her coat, Megan bustled around the kitchen, trying to keep her mind from straying to her husband. Why did it matter to her that he didn't act toward her like a husband should act toward a wife? She knew that no man would ever be attracted to her, didn't she? She'd come to that conclusion long ago.

So why did she find herself longing for Jesse's touch? The memory of her father kissing her mother, the two of them snuggling together when they thought no one could see them, tugged at her heart. Although she'd never admitted it, she'd yearned for that kind of relationship with a man. What a joy it would be to have Jesse look at her the way Papa had looked at Momma—like she was the most precious jewel in the world.

A burst of cold air tumbled in as Jesse stamped through the door. With a glance, Megan noted his rosy cheeks and the look of good health that made him glow. He'd recovered from the pneumonia, much to her relief. For weeks he'd been weak; but he refused to rest, working long hours, doing any little job he could find that needed done. There were always things to be fixed on a farm.

"Thank you." Jesse clenched his fingers around the cup of coffee Megan handed him. She loved the strong look of him. He wasn't tall or slender like many of the boys and men she'd known. Instead, Jesse was as sturdy as an oak. He didn't have fat on him. He worked far too hard for that, but he was solid. Sometimes she had trouble keeping herself from touching his hands or finding out if his arms were as rocklike as they appeared.

"Thank you." Megan couldn't look up at him.

"For what?"

"For all you've done." She gestured in the direction of the newly filled graves. "For caring enough to see to their proper burial."

"You're welcome." Jesse took a gulp, then sputtered and nearly choked. "Whew, this isn't left over. I didn't expect it to be so hot." He flashed a smile. "I want to take you to church tomorrow."

"But we can't." Megan backed up a step.

"The roads are passable. I've made sure all the tack is mended. If we leave early, we'll be able to get there on time."

Megan's heart pounded. Facing Mr. Sparks at the bank had been bad enough. To face the whole congregation, knowing what they thought she'd done, was more than she could do. "What about Seana? She'll get chilled."

"We'll wrap her up good. You can heat some rocks in the fireplace to keep her feet warm. I'll pack them around her myself." Jesse set the cup on the table. "My mind's made up, Megan. We need to go to church. I know why you don't want to go, but you have to face them sometime. If they're good Christian people, they'll be glad to see you."

❧

Clucking to the tired team, Jesse noted the number of wagons and carriages surrounding the small church at the outskirts of Yankton. He tried to ignore Megan's pallor as her whitened fingers gripped the seat beside him. Since the beginning of the marriage, he'd wanted to ask her about the comments made by Reverend Porter and his wife, but he hadn't been sure he'd even heard them right. Everything about that day faded into fuzziness as he tried to pin his thoughts down. He'd been so sick, he hadn't realized he was married until Seana said something. He could still recall the shock as reality took hold. Megan was his wife, although still in name only. For some reason he'd sensed fear and uncertainty in her. As much as he longed for a closer relationship, he wanted to wait until she was ready.

In almost every way, Megan was the opposite of Sara, the girl to whom he'd been betrothed. Where Sara was tall and slender, Megan was short and well rounded. Sara's blond locks and fair complexion contrasted completely with Megan's mahogany hair and sun-browned skin. Even on the inside they were opposites. Sara thought only of herself and what others could do for her. Megan always thought of others first. Her constant attention to his every need testified to that. After knowing Megan, Jesse couldn't believe he'd ever been attracted to Sara. Of course, much of that attraction had been the result of his parents' insistence that she would be right for him. How wrong they had been.

"Are we there, Meggie?" Seana rose up on her knees to peer between them. Excitement made her eyes sparkle more than they had in some time.

"We're here." Megan's short response spoke volumes of her reluctance to face these people. Jesse wanted to help her, but he knew it was best for her to face her fears. That's why he had made her come. When she saw how friendly these people would be, she'd relax and enjoy the fellowship.

The tinny plink of a piano drifted from inside the building as Jesse hopped down to secure the team. By the time they walked up the steps to the door, the hymn was in full swing, the chorus of voices echoing the song in his heart. Oh, how he'd missed the fellowship with other believers. If only this church were close enough to attend every week.

Megan had a tight hold on Seana's shoulder. Jesse wasn't sure if she didn't want the girl to skip on ahead or if she needed the support. He took Megan's elbow in his hand, guiding her into the sanctuary. The floorboards creaked. The people sitting closest to the door glanced around. One by one they stopped singing and stared at the Coulters. Jesse urged Megan to continue down the aisle where there were empty seats. As they passed the rows, silence descended, except for one group of young people about Megan's age. One of the girls leaned over to whisper to her companion. Before the Coulters passed them, the whole group was staring at Megan and snickering. Megan acted as if she hadn't noticed, but Jesse could see the flush in her cheeks. By the time they arrived at the empty pew, even the pianist stopped playing, the air filled with silent tension.

Her face bright red, Megan stared at the floor. Jesse smiled at the grim faces around him. Reverend Porter, standing at the front of the congregation in a black suit that gave him the appearance of a vulture, stared at them with narrowed eyes. An uncomfortable silence stretched until Jesse thought he might explode.

Reverend Porter nodded. "It's nice to see the Coulters here this Sunday. Mrs. Porter, perhaps we could start this hymn over again."

Jesse couldn't begin to imagine the cause for the animosity he felt from these people. Mrs. Porter, seated at the piano, began to pound the keys with a force that threatened to ruin the instrument. This time the singing lacked conviction. Under the guise of the music, Jesse could hear the whispers as ladies and gentlemen alike tilted their heads together and passed on some bit of gossip. He ground his teeth together in an effort to keep quiet.

As the hymn drew to a close, Reverend Porter gestured for his wife to take her seat in the pew near the piano. He smoothed his dark coat and opened a huge Bible. Clearing his throat, he read, " 'Whither shall I go from thy spirit? or whither shall I flee from thy presence? If I ascend up into heaven, thou art there: if I make my bed in hell, behold, thou art there.' " He stared in silence, his gaze roving over the congregation and coming to settle on Megan. "Reading from Psalm 139, written by David, King of Israel."

His gaze never leaving Megan's downcast face, Reverend Porter pointed his finger. "There is nowhere you can go to hide from God. He always knows where you've been and what you've done. Your sin cannot be hidden."

Jesse listened in astonishment as the preacher continued to berate the congregation with a variety of possible sins they couldn't hide from the Lord. He made no reference to the forgiveness that comes from confessing your sins to Him. Instead, he consigned them all to an eternity in hell for the wrongs they'd done—or had he? Most of his message was directed at Megan, or at least in her direction. What had she done that these people felt so much hostility toward her? She had the best heart of anyone he'd ever met. She didn't raise her voice to him, didn't argue, and didn't demand her own way, even though she'd been forced into a situation she didn't want. Why did this preacher condemn her?

"Is it adultery or fornication you've committed? In some secret place you thought no one would know about?" Reverend Porter's voice sounded more like the hiss of a serpent than that of a man of God. "Not only does God know your dirty secrets, but He tells His people to be set apart from sinners."

Reverend Porter straightened. "I suggest if you're one of those living in sin that you refrain from attending this church. We do not want the reputation of the Corinthian church. They willingly put up with disgusting sins until the apostle Paul set them straight. We will not tolerate sinful behavior here."

Megan's hands were clenched in her skirts. Jesse could tell from the set of her shoulders that she was strung like a tight wire ready to snap. Anger filled him at the injustice of this man condemning someone rather than extending the forgiveness of Jesus. Who taught Porter about the Bible? They hadn't done a very good job. He couldn't wait to leave here. If he'd known the bigotry they would face, he would never have subjected Megan to this travesty.

The church meeting ended with a sonorous prayer by Reverend Porter, extolling the virtues of living a sinless life and condemning those who didn't. Jesse gritted his teeth. Reaching down, he covered Megan's clenched fist with his hand. He felt her start, and he could feel her trembling, most likely from the same anger that consumed him.

Outside, the congregation separated into small groups, speaking in hushed whispers and staring at the door of the church as the Coulters stepped out. Jesse still held Megan's hand. She seemed to be drawing strength from him. For the first time since their arrival, she lifted her chin and straightened. She didn't meet the gaze of any of the people clustered around, but stared off across the wide lawn toward where their wagon awaited. Jesse wondered if she were judging the distance and the time it would take them to cross over and be gone from here. He couldn't blame her at all. He wanted to leave this place and never return.

They were almost to the wagon when a voice halted them. "Megan, wait." Glancing over his shoulder, Jesse saw a short, heavyset woman hurrying to catch them. In her arms she cradled a sleeping baby. Four children trailed after her like quail after a mama. By the time she reached them, she had to gasp for breath before she could speak. Megan stiffened as if terrified of what the woman would say.

"Megan, Dear, I'm so glad we both came to church today. This is the first time we've been here since the blizzard." Her voice trailed off. Tears sparkled in her eyes. "I just wanted to tell you how sorry we are about your family and what happened. If there's anything William and I can do, please say so."

Megan relaxed. "Thank you, Mrs. Bright. I'm sorry I haven't been by to visit, but the weather has been bad." An awkward silence fell. "I don't believe you've met my husband, Jesse Coulter. Jesse, this is one of our neighbors, Mrs. Edith Bright."

"Mr. Coulter, it's a pleasure to meet you. Oh, there's William coming with the reverend. If you're like us, you have to head back right away. Perhaps we could travel together and stop along the way for our lunch." Edith raised her hand to wave at the approaching men. She didn't seem to be aware of the dark cloud hovering around the preacher.

nine

Dread filled Megan as she watched the preacher stalking toward her. This day looked like it might go from bad to worse. After the way Reverend Porter's gaze bored into her in church and the reaction of the congregation when she, Jesse, and Seana walked in, she knew the angry frown on Reverend Porter's face boded ill. She pasted on a smile as she smoothed the ruffle along Seana's collar.

"Good afternoon, Mr. Bright, Reverend Porter." Megan hoped they couldn't see how much she wanted to turn and run. She tightened her hold on Jesse's hand, almost unaware of doing so.

"I don't know what you're doing, showing your face here like this. Did you think we wouldn't have heard about your meeting with Mr. Sparks?" Reverend Porter said.

"What are you talking about?" Megan glanced at Jesse. He seemed as puzzled as she did.

"Mr. Sparks told me about you coming to town on the pretense of asking about the loan. Any decent Christian wouldn't have proposed what you did while your husband waited outside. Although reluctant to believe the rumors we'd heard about you, after talking with our esteemed banker, I can see they were true."

"Exactly what did I say to Mr. Sparks?" Megan tried to push away the feelings of impending doom. She wanted to climb in the wagon and drive away from here as fast as possible. Would she never be free of the vicious lies those young men told about her?

The preacher leaned over and glared at Megan. "I'm talking about how you told Mr. Sparks you regretted not choosing him for a husband. You even suggested the two of you could meet privately on occasion."

Edith's gasp echoed Megan's. "I said no such thing. In fact, I didn't speak to Mr. Sparks without my husband there." Megan paled as she remembered Mr. Sparks calling her back as they were leaving. He said he wanted a private word, then only offered again his condolences about her parents. Jesse had been right outside the open door. She hadn't thought anything of the interchange.

"Don't add lying to your list of other sins, Mrs. Coulter."

"Just a minute, now." Jesse stepped forward, pushing between Megan and Reverend Porter. "I was at the bank, too. When Megan spoke to Mr. Sparks *privately,* I was right outside the door watching them. Mr. Sparks asked to speak to her, not the other way around. I believe you should question your source before accusing my wife of anything." Jesse's fists balled at his sides, his whole body like a tight spring. A thrill raced through Megan as she realized no one had ever stood up for her like this before. In spite of the accusations, she wanted to smile.

"We've known the Rileys for several years now." William Bright stepped forward. "Megan has never done anything to deserve such treatment. I think you could have at least given her the opportunity to tell her side of the story."

Reverend Porter whirled on Mr. Bright. "You're stuck out there in the middle of nowhere. You don't hear the things I hear. This girl has a sinful reputation that's followed her here. Now we're seeing her true colors. As a member of my congregation, I'm going to have to ask you and your missus to not associate with her."

Mr. Bright's jaw tightened. "I don't believe you have the authority to tell me who I can or can't associate with. The Rileys were a fine couple. I intend to stand by their daughter. Lee Riley helped me out more than once, and Megan, here, stayed with us when Edith had so much trouble with the last baby. I don't know what we'd have done without her help. She's a fine girl."

"Her parents told me they had to move out here to escape all the problems she caused with young men. At least out here they were away from town and so could keep her in line."

"Reverend, I've never hit a preacher in my life, but if you don't turn around and leave us, you're going to be the first. If I'm not mistaken, you're gossiping about information told to you in private. In my Bible, gossip is a sin." Jesse tilted forward until his face was inches from Porter's. All across the grounds, people were silent as they watched the interchange.

The two men glared at each other for a long minute before Reverend Porter stepped back, easing the tension. Megan thought Jesse wanted to go after him, so she placed a hand on Jesse's arm. He glanced down. She gave a small smile. She could feel the muscles in his arm loosen. Taking her hand in his once again, Jesse faced the preacher. "You stopped a little too soon when you were reading from Psalm 139. What about the next two verses? 'If I take the wings of the morning, and dwell in the uttermost parts of the sea; Even there shall thy hand lead me, and thy right hand shall hold me.' I guess that part of the Scripture didn't fit what you wanted to say. That psalm isn't talking about hiding our sin as much as letting us know that God is always there to guide us. No matter where we go, He'll lead us if we allow Him."

Turning his back on the preacher, Jesse led Megan and Seana to the wagon. He handed them both up, then turned to Mr. Bright. "I don't believe we've been introduced, Mr. Bright. I'm Jesse Coulter, Megan's husband. We'd take it kindly if you would join us on the trip home. Megan has some lunch packed."

"I do, too." Edith Bright, surrounded by her wide-eyed children, took a step closer. "We can stop and combine our lunches. The company will be enjoyable." She sent a glare at the preacher.

"You go on ahead. I'll get my family loaded up." William Bright shook Jesse's hand. "If we're going to be neighbors, I'd like to get to know you. Living so far from town, we have to stick together." He, too, shot an angry look at the departing preacher, raising his voice on the last words so they would be heard by anyone close.

"Meggie, can I ride with Sally?" Seana enjoyed the rare visits she got with the oldest Bright girl. "Please?" At Edith's nod, Megan gave her permission and watched as her sister clambered down and skipped over to climb into the Brights' wagon, giggling with her friend as if there weren't any troubles in the world.

The small groups of people scattered around the church grounds began whispering together, their glances raking over Megan. Jesse clicked his tongue, and the horses began to move. Megan held her head high, unwilling to allow these people to know how upset she was. On the way home, she should explain to Jesse why there were so many rumors about her. She didn't know if she had the courage to bring up her painful past.

❧

The horses snorted and tossed their heads as they drove away from Yankton. Jesse knew they were sensing the roiling emotions running through him. How could Reverend Porter call himself a Christian, yet treat someone the way he'd treated Megan? There were places in Scripture talking about discipline in the church, but this wasn't the way to handle it. Reverend Porter should have come to the house with Mr. Sparks in tow to talk to Megan, rather than confronting her in front of the whole congregation as if she were some common criminal unworthy of justice.

Besides, where had the esteemed Mr. Sparks been today? Wasn't he a member of this church? If he didn't even attend Sunday services, then Reverend Porter should certainly give Megan the benefit of the doubt, considering she and her family always attended when they could.

For the first mile, he allowed his feelings to stew, glancing back once to find the Brights about an eighth of a mile behind them. Megan sat board stiff beside him on the seat, her gaze straight ahead. He wanted to talk to her, but he didn't know how to start. Since their marriage, they'd only talked of farm-related concerns. The realization dawned that they hadn't ever talked about anything husbands and wives usually shared. He found he wanted to tell her about his call to be a pastor, and he wanted to know her likes and dislikes. He especially wanted to know what had hurt her so much and what dark cloud followed her when she moved out West with her parents.

A quiet sniff broke his concentration. From the corner of his eye, he could see the way Megan's fingers trembled as they clasped together in her lap. From the movement of the material in her dress, he knew her whole body shook with her effort to hold in her hurt. A single tear rolled down her cheek, but she still didn't relax or let her gaze drift his way.

The horses were going on their own now. They'd been over this road often enough to know the way home. Jesse loosened his grip on the reins. The tension and anger inside him flowed away, replaced with compassion and caring for his wife, something that he'd never expected to feel. Shifting the reins to one hand, he put his other arm around Megan's shoulder and drew her close. She resisted for a moment, then leaned her head against his shoulder.

Jesse marveled at how natural it felt to have Megan leaning against him. Her head fit just right in the curve of his shoulder. Closing his eyes, he breathed deeply, loving the scent of soap mixed with the fresh smell of outdoors and sun. He wanted to rest his cheek on her head, to caress her arm. He wanted to kiss her and care for her as a true husband should.

"Megan, I'm so sorry I made you go to church. I had no idea you would be treated that way." Jesse stroked her arm.

She shuddered. With a sob, she erupted in tears. He held

her tight until the crying eased, murmuring soft words of comfort, praying God would guide him as a husband.

"I'm sorry." Megan pushed away from him, wiping at her cheeks. "I don't usually act like this."

"You don't usually get attacked in front of a crowd of people." Jesse pulled out his handkerchief and offered it to her. "I've never known a preacher to be so vicious."

"I've seen him do worse." Megan gave a slight hiccup as she wiped her eyes.

"Worse than this?"

Megan nodded. "A few years ago we had a family in town whose boys were. . .rambunctious." She glanced up at Jesse with reddened eyes. "The boys weren't bad; they were full of energy and life. They liked to play practical jokes, and some people didn't like that. Reverend Porter has always been stern and doesn't see amusement in much of anything."

She paused to blow her nose. "Anyway, the boys played a practical joke on the Porters. It was harmless, but the reverend took offense. He called the parents up in front of the congregation the next Sunday and chastised them for not having control of their children. He read Scripture, although much of it out of context, according to my father. By the time he finished, the family was so humiliated, they left."

"They left town or church?"

"Church that morning. They tried to stay in town, but Reverend Porter has a lot of influence here. So many people were against them, the family ended up leaving. I only hope they found a good church and a pastor who will not be so condemning.

"Papa often said if there was any other church to attend, he would change in an instant. I know of others who agreed with him."

"I suppose there aren't any other churches close enough to ride to." Jesse pursed his mouth in thought. A seed of an idea began to sprout.

"No." Megan glanced behind them, a thoughtful expression on her face. "You know, you have a lot of knowledge of the Bible. Seana and I both appreciate the lessons you've done on the Sundays we stayed home." She fell quiet, nibbling at her bottom lip.

"What if—"

"I've been thinking—"

Megan blushed as she and Jesse both spoke at once. Jesse flashed her a grin. "Go ahead, you first."

She hesitated, smoothing her skirt with her gloved hands. "What if you started a church? I guess that would never work because we live so far from town, but I think a lot of people around here would welcome someone other than Reverend Porter. If only we weren't so far from Yankton."

Jesse nodded. "That's sort of what I wanted to talk to you about." He took her hand, needing the contact. She didn't pull away. "I've been thinking about how we don't really know each other. Ever since the wedding, we've talked about Seana or the farm, but we've never learned much about one another." He paused as she looked away. Had he seen a look of fear in her eyes? What was she afraid of?

"Yoo-hoo, Megan." Mrs. Bright called from behind them.

Jesse hadn't realized how close the neighbors had gotten to them. They must have pushed their team some to catch up. He tried not to show his disappointment. They could talk later. Jesse hauled on the reins, pulling the horses to a halt. He and Megan both turned in their seats to face the Brights.

"Megan, these boys are just about to starve to death." Mrs. Bright's laugh tinkled in the chilly air. "I think that includes William. Men and boys are always hungry. Are you and Jesse ready to stop for a bite to eat?"

Glancing first at Jesse, Megan pointed at a small rise of land. "We're ready. Momma and Papa used to have lunch at the next rise. The ground will be a little drier there. Is that okay?"

"Lead on." William clucked to his team at the same time

Jesse did. The wagons rattled along the road for a few minutes to the small hill.

As soon as they halted, the children tumbled over the side of the wagon and scampered to the top of the hill. Seana and Sally climbed at a more sedate pace, the pair still in deep conversation. Jesse smiled, remembering how his sisters and their friends giggled and talked for hours.

Handing Megan a blanket, Jesse lifted the basket of food from the back of the wagon. One of the many things he appreciated about Megan was her cooking skill. Without the hard work needed to keep up a farm, he would be as fat as one of their hogs by now. She made the lightest biscuits and the tastiest stew he'd ever eaten. He knew she had packed a fried chicken in the lunch this morning, and his mouth watered at the thought.

"Here, let me take that." Megan stretched out her hand for the blankets Edith Bright was juggling along with the baby.

"Do you want the blankets or Henry?" Edith asked. "If you don't mind, I'd love a break from this one. He's done nothing but squirm all the way from town."

Megan held out her arms. Henry gurgled as he almost jumped at her. The look of utter delight on Megan's face as she cuddled the wiggling infant close in her arms told Jesse she would make a great mother. He'd never given much thought to being a father; but watching Megan, his heart filled with a longing so strong, he thought anyone would be able to see.

As the women strolled up the rise after the children, William stepped up beside Jesse, lugging a much bigger basket. "I heard in town that you're about to lose the farm. Sometime soon I'd like to talk about Mr. Sparks and the shenanigans he's pulling around here. Something just doesn't smell right."

ten

Before the man had a chance to say more, Edith called for them to hurry up and bring the food. The older boys raced back and forth between their parents as Jesse and William climbed the hill, toting the baskets. The two boys were full of energy, as only the young possessed. They settled down when the food was laid out, however, and everyone dug into the food with gusto.

"More chicken?" Megan lifted the bowl, still half full of fried chicken, and offered it to Jesse. He shook his head, then sighed.

"You're going to fatten me up, Megan. I think there is one more piece calling my name." Jesse felt a thrill of satisfaction at Megan's blush. "I don't know how I managed to be the one to have you as a wife." He leaned forward, noting the Brights were taking care of a fight between the boys. "You are a blessing." He winked. Megan's cheeks turned bright red. Jesse snatched a chicken leg from the bowl and took a big bite to hide his grin. He didn't want her to think him insincere, but he couldn't help being delighted to watch her. Giving her a compliment was like watching a rose blossom. He knew her parents were very good and loved her. The uncertainty must come from whatever hurt she'd endured before they moved here. He hoped someday she would be able to get past that pain.

"Jesse, we've heard you're from the Chicago area." Edith gave a frazzled smile, relaxing as her boys calmed down. "Do you still have family there?"

"Yes, Ma'am. My parents and two sisters still live there. Both of my sisters are married."

"Whatever made you decide to ride out West—and in the

middle of the winter?" Edith served William a piece of chocolate cake.

"I. . .I guess I needed to get away for awhile." Jesse knew the excuse sounded lame. He didn't know these people well enough to go into detail about his personal life and failures. He wasn't even sure if he could share that with Megan, yet he felt he would have to, soon. "I didn't think about getting caught in a blizzard, though. I guess I should have waited until spring."

William scooped up the baby before he rolled into the cake. The tot chortled. William grinned. "Were you headed to Lead or Deadwood? I heard you planned to work in the gold fields."

"I hadn't actually decided which town to settle in. I thought I'd wait and get a feel for the place." Jesse began helping Megan pack up the lunch items. He didn't want to admit that his going out West had been a result of running from God, not a desire for adventure, as most people thought.

Giving the baby to Sally, William began helping Edith pack up their basket. The boys, faces pocked with chocolate cake crumbs, darted away across the rise, running as fast as their little legs could move. The baby let out a squall as Sally rocked him in her arms. Edith held out her hands for the screaming infant.

"Edith, why don't you and Megan sit here and visit while Jesse and I carry the baskets to the wagon? We can take a few minutes before we have to leave."

Jesse felt his stomach clench. He nodded his agreement to Megan and strode toward the wagon, the lighter basket clasped in his hand. He hoped William would have some sort of information he could use to help them get out of debt and keep the farm. He knew how much this meant to Megan, and now it meant a lot to him, too. He'd come to love this place, with its rolling hills and wide-open spaces. This wasn't at all like Chicago, where people were packed like animals in a pen. Neighbors were nice once in awhile, but he liked being able to go outside and stretch without everyone in a five-mile radius hearing about it.

Both baskets landed in their respective wagons with audible thumps. Jesse walked back to help William check the harnesses on his horses. He didn't know how to broach the subject, so he waited for the older man to speak first.

William cleared his throat. He ran expert hands over the traces and buckles, but Jesse could see his mind wasn't on the harnesses or horses.

"First the Sheffields, then the Murrays, the Reids, the Overtons, and last of all the Baxters." William leaned his arms over his horse's back as he stared at Jesse. "Those are the farmers who've had Sparks foreclose on their land in the last six months. Most of them were gone before anyone knew what had happened. I've heard the sheriff accompanies Sparks and escorts the family off their land before they even have a chance to pack much of anything."

"Why are so many people taking out loans they can't pay off? Have the crops been bad?"

William stared off into the distance. "I didn't know any of the families that well, except Megan's folks and Patrick Murray. They had the farm just past ours. Patrick and I talked on occasion, and the wives enjoyed getting together for a visit. Patrick mentioned having a loan, but I thought he said he paid it off with the proceeds from last year's crops. In fact, he had an exceptional year and said he would be ahead some because of it."

William combed his fingers through the horse's mane. "I know because, after harvest, he and his wife invited us over for a little celebration. He said this year would be the first he wouldn't have to borrow money for seed."

"So what happened?"

William shrugged. "I don't know. I went over one day a

couple of months later. The house was deserted. Some of their belongings were still there, but no one had lived in the house for a long time. I rode to town, thinking something bad might have happened to them. The sheriff said they defaulted on their loan and had to be evicted. He heard they'd gone on west, but he didn't know where."

"I'd have thought they'd have contacted you before they left."

"I know." William gave the horse's neck an affectionate slap and led the way to Jesse's team. "That's when I remembered hearing about others being evicted. I asked some discreet questions and found out about the others I mentioned. There may have been more I haven't heard about. This is a big territory. Communication isn't always the best."

Jesse nodded, lost in thoughts of his own. Was this banker involved in something underhanded? If so, how would he ever prove that? He couldn't even find the papers from the loan Megan's father took out.

The chatter of the women and the squeals of the children drew Jesse back. He finished readying the horses and felt William's hand on his shoulder.

"Watch yourself, Jesse. I knew Lee Riley pretty well. I don't recall him ever saying anything about a loan he owed the bank that was due this spring."

The next few minutes passed in a flurry as women and children said good-bye and loaded into the wagons. In another few miles they would be parting ways and probably wouldn't see one another for at least a month. Unease filled Jesse as he thought of how little time he had to solve this dilemma before the sheriff paid them a visit and they wouldn't have a home anymore.

❧

The soft crackle of the fire soothed Megan as she relaxed in the rocking chair. Despite the difficult time at church, this had proved to be a wonderful day. She hadn't realized how much she missed another woman's company until she had the chance to visit with Edith. When she'd stayed with them last year, she and Edith had become very close. She loved those little rascals, too, and Sally.

The rhythmic scrape of Jesse sharpening knives, completing his evening chore, reminded her so much of her father that for a moment tears blinded her. Jesse worked so hard for her and Seana.

For the first time since they'd arrived home, she allowed herself the luxury of remembering the way Jesse stood up for her at church today. When they first walked into the church, she felt the animosity. She knew the instant Reverend Porter saw them and hadn't thought she could continue walking down the aisle. Then Jesse took her elbow, and strength she didn't know she had suffused her. She'd walked to that pew doing her best to ignore the townspeople who knew her terrible secret, or at least whatever version of that experience that had been spread about. Most likely the story didn't contain an ounce of truth.

The whole service had been directed at her, the sinful woman who dared to disrupt the meeting. She'd always felt sorry for those who had Reverend Porter's ire directed at them, and now she knew why. The man didn't know how to show any godly compassion. He passed judgment instead as if it were his God-given right to do so.

When they drove away from Yankton, she wanted to have the earth swallow her up. She didn't know how she could face anyone again, let alone her husband and her friends. Her body ached with the effort to hold in her feelings; but like a loose end, the thread of her emotions began to unravel. Then Jesse slipped an arm around her, urging her without a word to lean against him. He hadn't said anything, just let her cry while he comforted her. He hadn't asked why people treated her so poorly. He'd never asked about any of the references to her ruined reputation. He'd simply shown her God's love. She'd never had any man comfort her like that since she'd grown too old to sit on her father's lap. Something inside her warmed at the idea that Jesse might see her differently than others did.

On the way home after lunch, Jesse had continued to hold her hand, as if he wanted to have contact with her. From the feelings fluttering through her as his thumb circled on the back of her hand, Megan couldn't imagine what it would be like if they hadn't been wearing gloves. The thought made her flush. She ducked her head, hoping Jesse wouldn't notice and wonder what she was thinking.

She'd expected Jesse to notice the girls in town, but he hadn't. He hadn't even glanced at Belinda Parkins, with her gorgeous blond hair and slender figure. All the boys fought for the opportunity to sit with her. Even many of the older men earned angry nudges from their wives when Belinda walked past. Belinda had always been the one to laugh at Megan for her "cute chubbiness," making all the others their age laugh while Megan wanted to die. That's why she didn't enjoy trips to town or attending church.

Jesse sighed and arched his back, which must ache from bending over so long. He checked the edge of the knife blade and nodded. Picking up his sharpening stone and rags, he took them to his room to put them away. She could never fault Jesse for being messy. Like her father, Jesse always cleaned up after himself. She appreciated that.

"I don't suppose I could convince you to stop your mending for awhile." Jesse stood in the doorway smiling at her. Megan's heart thudded.

"Is there something you want me to do?"

"Yep." He grinned, his cinnamon eyes twinkling dark in the firelight. "Since Seana seems to be asleep, I'd like you to take a walk with me. I know it's cold, but we could check on the livestock and look at the stars."

Her breath caught in her throat. She didn't think she could answer. Stabbing the needle into the cloth, she set the piece aside before she hurt herself. Why did he want to walk with her? Did he plan to tell her he was leaving?

He must have taken her setting the mending aside as a yes, because he clomped to the door and plucked her coat from the peg. "Here you go." He held out the garment, waiting for her to put it on. Megan wasn't sure if she wanted to go along with this, but as she looked at Jesse, she couldn't see how she could say no. He'd been so kind and gallant today. How could she ruin that?

The night was clear and cold. Millions of stars shone against the black sky, some twinkling like tiny fireflies in the heavens. Her breath whooshed out white on the air, even after passing through her scarf. The last remnants of snow clung in dirty patches to the places that received the most shade during the day. Soon the snow would be gone and spring would arrive. The hills would be covered in green and dotted with bright flowers. She loved that time of year.

Jesse threaded her hand around the crook in his elbow and led the way to the barn. Tingles ran through Megan at the contact. Never before had he shown this desire to touch her. Why was he doing so now?

The warm, damp smell of livestock and hay greeted them when Jesse opened the barn door. At one end a sow grunted at the intrusion of light from the lantern Jesse carried. The horses snorted and stamped. Jesse's gelding moved to the front of his stall and gave a soft whicker of greeting to his master.

"They all look okay." Megan jarred the stillness with her words. She felt she had to say something.

Jesse smiled down at her. "Then let's go for a little walk. That is, if you can stand the cold."

"Sure." Megan tried to keep the apprehension from her tone. The night air chased away any shadows of exhaustion from the long day. She'd always loved the nights here. No factory smoke tinted the sky. The quiet spoke to her as if God Himself would come down here and walk with her. She'd always loved the feeling, but had never shared it with someone else.

The crunch of frozen ground told of their passing as they walked. Jesse didn't say anything, but he brought his arm closer to his side, tugging her along, too. She thought about removing her hand from his grip, but knew she didn't want to.

"Have you ever had a beau?" Jesse's question took her breath away. Had he heard rumors of what had happened? A tremor raced through her.

"No, I haven't." Her voice shook. "We don't get out much, and we live so far from town." She walked faster, not sure what she wanted him to believe.

Pulling her to a stop, Jesse turned to face her. He hadn't let go of her hand, but now took both hands in his. "Megan, I have something I want to say to you." He gazed up at the stars, his lips tight together as if he were trying to figure out how to phrase something.

"On the way home today, I realized that we haven't spent any time getting to know one another." He squeezed her hand, and she stopped what she was about to say. "I want to learn about who you are. There are things you need to know about me, too. I know we didn't plan to get married, but to me marriage is forever. If you're to be my wife, I want to know all about you."

Fear blazed through Megan. Would he want to know about her shame?

"Hey." Jesse waited until she looked up. "I know something happened to you before you moved out here. You don't need to tell me about it if you don't want to. Whatever it was, I know that right now you're a wonderful, caring person. I've seen the way you are with Seana, the way you held that baby today. You were so hurt by your parents' and brother's deaths, yet you've carried on in a remarkable way. I admire you, Megan."

She stood frozen, staring up at him. What was he saying?

"Megan, I've come to care about you." Jesse drew her even closer. His arms closed around her, and she wondered if he could feel her pulse pounding.

"I like the way you look. You're not skinny and wasted like some girls. You aren't whiny or self-centered. I like the way you feel in my arms." His voice trailed off. He bent his head and touched his lips to hers. Megan clung to him, wishing this moment could last forever.

eleven

Quiet rang through the house. A few night birds called to one another outside, disturbing the late night peace. Seana's soft breathing in the bed across the room gave the only whisper of sound inside. Megan touched a fingertip to her lips, marveling at the remembered feel of Jesse's kiss. Conflicting feelings warred inside her. Would he, too, betray her and ridicule her? Hope flared up, fighting the negative emotions that threatened to drag her down. She'd felt hope before, but that hadn't stopped what happened. At long last the heaviness in her limbs drew her down into an exhausted sleep.

The voices began calling. Laughing voices. Young people having fun. Megan turned to see a door, cracked open, a shaft of light pouring out, inviting all who passed to enter.

Her feet dragged at the ground as she drifted toward the door. The voices grew louder. Girlish giggles mingled with manly chuckles and laughter. The clink of glasses added a tinkling quality.

As Megan approached, the strip of light widened. Megan could see through the opening. Instead of a room, a green lawn stretched out before her. The grass sparkled and waved in the sunlight. Huge trees made a rustling noise as the wind wove through their leaves. A pond glittered at the far end of the sloping lawn.

Close to where Megan stood, a group of young people was seated at a long table. The girls wore party dresses, the boys, their good suits. A huge mound of food rested on a nearby table. The young people had well-laden plates before them, although the food looked untouched.

Dread crept over Megan in a nauseating wave. She recognized them. Turning around, she groped for the door, wanting to escape before they noticed her. The door had disappeared as if it had never been there in the first place. She was trapped.

"Did you see her?" Hiram spoke. Handsome, sought after, Hiram. The boy all the girls wanted to notice them. Somehow Megan faced them again. She wanted to move, but her body refused to respond.

"Tell me about it." Susan leaned toward Hiram, giving him a coquettish smile. "I want to hear the story again."

Hiram laughed, his head tipped back, his blond hair falling in waves from his perfect features. "How could she have thought I would be interested in her? Truly, by the time she has a child or two, she'll be the size of a cow." Hiram paused as his audience crowed in delight.

"She was the easiest girl to dupe."

"You mean you've done this before?" One of the other boys leaned forward, listening with obvious interest.

"Of course." Hiram waved his hand in the air. "These poor young things need someone to give them attention. I saw her at every church function and dance, standing to one side looking like some chubby, forlorn puppy." The group howled again.

"I just wanted to give her a little excitement." He leaned forward. His tone took on a hushed note. "I didn't know she would respond so. . .um, enthusiastically."

The other boys grinned and prodded one another with their elbows. The girls blushed, hiding for a moment behind their fans.

"How did you get through that crusty exterior?" the other boy asked. "When I tried to talk to her, she turned out to be as cold as a fish."

"It takes finesse." Hiram smoothed his hair. "You have to show just the right amount of interest, yet leave some mystique that draws her into the net. I've mastered the technique."

"So what did you do?" The eager boy grinned in anticipation.

"Well. . ." Hiram frowned and rubbed his chin as if deep in thought. "I became vulnerable." He grinned at their puzzled expressions. "I pretended to be hurt. As she was leaving, I opened the gate for her. In the process I managed to—on purpose—get a splinter in my palm. Women can't resist a wounded man." He chuckled. "By the time she assisted me in removing the splinter, she agreed when I insisted on walking her home. One thing led to another from there." He shrugged, as if the conquest had been nothing.

"No." Megan opened her mouth to scream, but no sound came out. "He's telling you lies. This isn't what happened." How many times had she tried to convince everyone that Hiram had lied? No one listened to her.

"Did you. . .did she. . . ?" The boy couldn't get his question out in his eagerness.

"Of course." Hiram polished his fingernails against his shirt. "You saw what she looked like when we caught up with all of you. How could you doubt what we'd been doing? She was still clinging to me. I could barely get away."

Horror encompassed Megan. Why did she have to hear these lies again? Tears streamed down her cheeks. Even her parents hadn't been sure of her innocence in the face of the lies Hiram told. She'd tried to explain how she'd tripped and tumbled down a hillside. That's how her dress got the mud on it and her hair so disheveled. She clung to Hiram's arm because her ankle throbbed from the fall.

Even the bruise that developed there didn't convince anyone that she'd told the truth. Everyone said she was desperate for a young man's attention and willing to do anything to get it. Megan had never known such shame.

"So do I have a chance with her, too?" The young man rubbed his palms on his pant legs.

"All of you have a chance." Hiram's eyes twinkled. "If you have no success, then you aren't half the man I think you are. Let us know," he called after him as the boy dashed away.

"No." Megan wept in uncontrollable sobs. She had to do something to stop this. She hadn't before, and look at the results. She tried to push forward, to confront Hiram, but her body refused to move. Twisting and turning, she cried out again and again.

"Meggie, Meggie, wake up." Seana's small hands gripped her shoulders, shaking her. Megan couldn't seem to stop the sobs. Her pillow felt damp from the crying she'd been doing while dreaming.

"What's going on?" Jesse called from outside the door. "I'm coming in."

After the nightmare she'd just experienced, Jesse should have been threatening to Megan, but somehow a measure of peace descended with his arrival. Seana moved aside, and Jesse sat down, pulling her into his arms like he might comfort a young child. For a long time he stroked her back, whispering soothing sounds that she couldn't even make into words.

"Seana, I want you to go on back to bed. Your sister's fine." Jesse spoke only after Megan's trembling eased. "I'm going to take Megan out and fix her some warm milk. You go on back to sleep."

Crawling back in bed, Seana was asleep almost before Jesse could tuck the covers around her. He turned back to

Megan and scooped her up, covers and all, and carried her out into the kitchen. She waited in silence, watching as he built a small fire in the stove to warm some milk for her.

The drink tasted delicious, warming her clear down to her toes. Her eyes opened in surprise at the touch of sugar he'd added. Her mother always added sweetener and cinnamon, but most people didn't. Even without the spice, the hot tonic was perfect.

"Thank you." Drowsiness overtook her almost before she took her last sip. She felt Jesse's strong arms lifting her from the chair as he carried her back to bed. The urge to talk to him, to tell him about the nightmare, plucked at her heart, but her tired body couldn't seem to respond. The gentle touch of his kiss on her forehead was the last thing she felt as she drifted off.

❧

For a long time, Jesse sat at Megan's bedside, watching her sleep. He'd never felt such tenderness for another person. When he awoke from a sound slumber to hear sobbing, he couldn't imagine what was wrong. Hearing Seana cry out for Megan made him move faster than he thought possible. The sight of her white face awash in tears haunted him. All he'd wanted to do was hold her and keep her safe from whatever followed after her.

"God." His words were barely audible in the quiet. "Please help me to be a good husband to Megan. Help her to trust me with whatever hurt she's suffered. Give me wisdom, Lord. I know You brought me here for a reason. Let me help her."

❧

The cows were lowing their protest by the time Jesse got to the barn next morning. "Sorry, girls." He patted the closest one on the rump. "Last night was a rough one. I missed the rooster this morning." He chuckled, wondering how anyone could rely on one of those feathered creatures that crowed whenever they felt like it, not just at the crack of dawn.

The quiet swish of milk into the pail brought out Mama Kitty. Jesse shot a stream of milk in her direction, which she lapped right out of the air. Shadow watched from the side, but didn't approach Jesse and the cow. When Mama Kitty began to clean her multicolored coat, Jesse lost interest and his thoughts turned to Megan. She'd looked so tired this morning. He wanted to tell her to go back to bed and get some rest, but he knew she wouldn't listen.

He set the milk pails near the door and began to fork hay into the feeders. The barn door creaked open. Megan stepped inside, pulling the door closed behind her. Jesse stopped, uncertain why she'd come out here. She usually fixed breakfast while he did the outside chores. She smiled, a rather strained one, but a smile nonetheless.

"Don't worry, I have Seana working on breakfast. I think she can fry a little bacon without burning it, and the biscuits are in the oven." She took a couple of hesitant steps. "Can we talk for a few minutes?"

Shoving the pitchfork into the pile of hay, Jesse gestured at a small bench. He tried to give her a smile that would put her at ease. "I can't think of anyone else I'd rather be talking to."

Megan blushed and ducked her head. She perched on the edge of the bench as if she wanted a quick getaway. She took off her mittens, and her fingers kneaded her coat buttons. "Thank you for last night. The milk and all. . ." She cleared her throat and looked away for a moment. "You said you wanted to learn more about me."

He covered her fidgeting fingers with his hand. "You don't have to tell me if you don't want to, Megan. But I want you to know I'm willing to listen if you do want to talk."

"I wanted to tell you last night, but I got so tired. The nightmare and all the old fears wore me out, I guess. Will you listen to the story now?"

He nodded.

"It isn't pretty. I want you to know that if you want to leave after hearing what I have to say, I'll understand." Her voice caught. She closed her eyes for a moment.

Leaning back against the stall behind them, Jesse slipped his arm around her shoulders. With a gentle tug, he leaned Megan back against his chest. This way she wouldn't have to face him, and it might be easier for her to tell the story.

In almost a monotone, Megan told him about the dream. She told him what happened, how no one believed or listened to her. Jesse felt her anguish and burned with anger at the young men who did this as a prank.

"Just that easily, my reputation was ruined. Hiram's lie cost me any hope of being treated decently. Even though I didn't accompany any of the other boys involved, they reported that I had. Rumors flew all over town. The pastor from our church came calling." Megan paused, lost in thought, her body strung as tight as the strings on a fiddle. "He looked like the Grim Reaper, and when he got done talking with my parents, they looked the same. It wasn't long after that when Papa announced we were selling our house and moving to the Dakota Territory."

Jesse tightened his arm around her. Her story hadn't turned him away. Instead, he wanted all the more to show her the love she deserved. She began to speak again, and he leaned forward to catch the soft words.

"In the last two months, I've thought often how I could be the cause for their deaths. If I hadn't been so blinded by that cad Hiram's good looks and sweet words in the first place, I'd never have gone with him. Then those boys never would have lied, and my family would never have had to leave."

"Megan, don't you do this." Jesse put his hands on her shoulders and turned her to face him. "Don't you ever blame yourself for what happened to your family. None of you could have predicted that blizzard."

She nodded. "I know. I guess sometimes I just feel sorry for myself." She shrugged. "That's not a very Christian way to act."

He brushed a piece of hay from her hair. "Maybe not, but it's very human." He stood and helped her to her feet. "I'd better finish these chores before Seana eats all that bacon she's cooking, and I don't get any."

"I meant what I said, you know." Megan stepped away from him, her hands twisting her coat.

"And what's that?" Jesse had no idea what she meant.

"I won't make you stay here. You were forced to marry me when you didn't even know what you were doing."

"Wait right there." Jesse held up a hand. "I may not have known, but God did. He's the one in charge of my life. I believe you're the right wife for me."

Tears glittered in her eyes. "I'm fat. I'm ugly. Why would you want to stay with me? You're so handsome. There are other prettier girls who would love to marry you."

"That is the last time I ever want to hear those words coming from your mouth." Jesse couldn't keep the anger from his voice. Megan looked up, wide-eyed.

"Megan, you are a masterpiece created by God." He lowered his voice. "He knit you together and made you who you are. You are perfect for me. God knew that." He wiped a tear from her cheek.

"One of the things I prayed after leaving home was that if God wanted me to marry, He would send a godly woman, just the right person for me. You, Megan, are that woman."

Tears were flowing unchecked down her face. Jesse pulled her close and pressed his lips against her hair. "I didn't have to marry you, Megan. I could have stayed in that bed and let them railroad you into marrying Mr. Sparks, but that wasn't God's plan. Can you see that?"

She nodded against his coat, and he stroked her back and her hair until she quieted in his arms. Tilting her chin up, Jesse smiled at her. Megan gave him a tentative smile.

"I think we'd better take the milk on in. What do you think? I can finish the chores here after breakfast."

Megan drew on her mittens and swiped at her cheeks with her mittened hands, nodding. Jesse followed her to the door, grabbing the bails of the buckets on his way. The sky was beginning to lighten in the east as they stepped outside. Jesse matched his steps to Megan's as they walked toward the house.

The door to the house flung open. Seana stumbled out. "Meggie, help me." A billow of smoke followed in her wake. Flames danced up the sleeves of Seana's dress, getting larger as the girl ran. Jesse's heart thudded as he quit thinking and sped toward Seana.

twelve

"Seana." Megan froze, staring in horror as her sister ran toward them. Flames leaped up her arms, reaching greedy fingers to her face and hair. Beside her, Jesse dropped the buckets with a clunk. The milk sloshed in the pails, but didn't spill over. Jesse raced for Seana, his feet churning up clumps of wet earth from the well-worn path.

Screams tore through the air. Megan's throat ached, and she knew she and Seana were both screaming. Jesse reached Seana and tackled her in midstride. He fell on top of her, covering her with his body. As if she'd suddenly been loosed from bondage, Megan leaped forward, her heart pounding. What was he doing? Jesse should be helping Seana, but he was going to hurt her worse than the fire!

Rolling back and forth, Jesse looked like he was forcing Seana deeper into the damp ground. Megan wanted to weep. Minutes before she'd trusted this man; now he was trying to kill her sister.

"Stop." Megan grasped Jesse by the collar of his coat and dragged at him. "Get off her. What are you doing?"

"Megan, it's okay." Jesse glanced back over his shoulder. "I'm not hurting her. It's what I had to do to get the fire completely out."

He rolled to the side. Seana's sobs turned to quiet hiccups. Mud coated much of her. Her hair was singed; and the smell of smoke, burnt clothing, and scorched flesh made Megan nauseous. Jesse lifted Seana up from the ground and hugged her to him. Megan realized he had tears on his cheeks. Where moments before she'd felt anger, now a fierce love poured through her. Jesse had saved Seana's life with his quick action.

"Take her." Jesse thrust Seana at Megan. He leapt away to snatch up the two pails of milk and dashed for the house. Megan and Seana hurried after him. Smoke still billowed from the doorway. Fear lodged in Megan's throat, making it difficult to swallow.

"Jesse." She trembled at the thought that he might be burned trying to put out the fire. She stopped in the doorway, letting her eyes adjust to the dimness and the billows of smoke. Across the room, Jesse stomped on embers burning into the wood planks of the floor. Moving fast, he rolled up the rag rug her mother had made and headed for the door. Megan stepped aside as he tossed the smoking rug into the yard.

Jesse turned to survey the room, his chest heaving, sweat beading on his brow. Megan began to cough. Her lungs burned with each breath she took. Beside her, Seana also began to cough.

"Take her out of here, Megan. This smoke isn't good to breathe."

Grabbing the sleeve of his coat, Megan stopped him as he started to cross the room. "You come, too. I don't want you to get hurt."

Jesse smiled and squeezed her hand. "You go on out. I'll be right there. I just want to check and make sure all the fire is out. Leave the door open to let the place air."

Holding her breath, Megan led Seana outside. Seana doubled over in a fit of coughing. By the time she finished, she was shaking so hard, she could barely stand. Megan led her to a bench along the wall of the house.

Easing the charred, sodden cloth away from Seana's arms, Megan had her first glimpse of the burns. They were bright red and already blistering. Smears of brown mud would need to be washed away. "Wait right here, Seana. I'll be back."

Going to the side of the house that saw the least sun, Megan dug through the mound of snow that bordered the edge. The crust had hardened, streaked with gray and black from the dirt. Underneath the crust, the snow was mostly clean. Megan scooped up a double handful and carried it back to her sister. Putting the snow on the bench beside Seana, Megan began to spread it over the singed flesh. She hoped this would stop the burning and cool Seana's arms. She also prayed the melting snow would help wash the dirt from the burns without doing further damage.

"It hurts, Meggie." Seana's sobs made Megan wish this pain could be hers instead. Why did this have to happen? Seana leaned forward and groaned as agony ripped through her. A few times Megan had received minor burns from cooking. From that experience, she could only imagine how painful these severe ones would be.

Megan was returning with her second handful of snow when Jesse stumbled from the house. He bent over on the stoop, hacking and gasping for air for a minute before he straightened.

"You're doing good." Jesse knelt beside Megan as she applied more snow to Seana's arms. "I'll get your coat, Seana, so you don't get too cold." He returned in a moment and draped the heavy outerwear over Seana's shaking shoulders. Megan felt like crying. How could she have forgotten how cold her sister must be? All she'd thought of was treating the wounds.

"You did fine." Jesse must have read her mind. His arm wrapped around her shoulders for a quick hug. "You needed to get the burns cooled off first. There's some salve in the barn that should help take the sting away and keep infection from setting in. I'll go get it as soon as you get her cleaned up enough."

"What happened?" Megan glanced up at Seana and Jesse as she realized things had been moving so fast she hadn't asked how the fire began.

"A log rolled out of the fireplace." Jesse sounded grim.

"It's my fault." Seana spoke so low, Megan wasn't sure she heard her.

"Nonsense." Megan looked up to see the tears swimming in Seana's eyes. "Sometimes the logs shift, and one will roll out. You know that's happened before. That's why we're careful to keep the rug away from the front of the fireplace."

"I don't think these logs shifted on their own." Jesse stared at Seana, who studied the ground.

"I did it." Seana looked at Megan, desperation in her gaze. "You were gone so long and the room was getting colder. I thought I could help by putting on a couple of logs. I knew you'd be cold and the warm fire would be nice. Then that one log moved and fell out. It rolled across the floor to the rug. I tried to roll it back, but my dress caught on fire." Her eyes filled with tears. "I'm sorry."

"Oh, Seana, I'm sorry, too." Megan leaned forward and kissed her sister's cheek. "I should have come back in the house sooner. I didn't mean to leave you for so long."

Seana glanced at Jesse. "I did get the biscuits out of the oven and I finished the bacon. At least you can have some breakfast."

Smiling, Jesse stood and swept her into his arms. "Then let's see if the smoke's cleared enough. I'm starving." He paused and gave Megan a sheepish grin. "I do hope we can just drink water today, though. I threw the milk on the fire to put it out."

Megan managed a smile. "I don't think I've ever heard of using milk that way."

❧

"Megan, I think we need to take Seana to town to see the doctor." Jesse stepped up behind Megan as she washed the breakfast dishes, speaking softly so Seana wouldn't hear him.

"Those burns are really bad. The doctor might have something to give her for the pain. I don't know if the salve I have will help enough, either."

Turning so her back was to her sister, Megan swallowed hard before speaking. "Couldn't you just ride to town and bring the doctor here? The trip might be too hard for Seana."

"That would take too long. I wouldn't get back before nightfall, and even that's not guaranteed. What if the doctor can't come right away?" Jesse brushed a stray lock of hair from Megan's face. "I know you don't like going to town, but for Seana, we have to. She isn't strong, anyway. I'm also worried about the smoke she breathed. She's still coughing, even though you and I stopped a long time ago."

Finishing the last of the dishes, Megan wiped her hands on a towel. Walking away from Jesse, she began to wash the table, swiping at nonexistent crumbs. Jesse had seen her clean the table already. He waited. She needed something to do while she considered their options.

"I've got some water warmed to wash her." Megan came to a stop beside him, but didn't look up.

"Don't make it too warm on her arms and face. Use cool water only on the burns. Don't rub, either."

Megan nodded. Jesse watched her face turn a little paler as she ladled water out of the kettle. He didn't know if she was worried about Seana and caring for her burns or if she was afraid of going to town. After Sunday's fiasco, he couldn't blame her for wanting to wait a long time before returning. Jesse knew Megan cared too much about Seana to forego seeing the doctor just because she didn't want to be seen in Yankton.

"I'll see to the stock and get the wagon hitched up while you're getting Seana ready to go." Jesse glanced down at his still-muddy clothing. "Then I'll come in and change before we leave." He touched Megan's shoulder. "I've seen someone burnt like this. They didn't get help, and the wounds got infected. I couldn't stand to see Seana go through something like that."

The drive to town seemed to take forever. Megan rode in back with Seana. Jesse had put down a mattress and several blankets to keep the young girl as comfortable as possible. Even so, the constant motion of the wagon caused her ceaseless pain. Megan had to keep Seana's arms uncovered so the blankets wouldn't pull any more skin away from her burns. Bits of cloth still clung to the worst of the injured areas. When Jesse tried to peel away her sleeves, the pain had been too great.

Lunchtime had passed when Jesse drove the wagon down the main street of town, following Megan's directions to the doctor's office. He felt bone weary. The travel wasn't as hard as knowing every jolt in the road hurt Seana. She'd passed out more than once on the trip here.

The doctor, a tall, thin man who looked more like an undertaker than a healer, took one look at Seana and motioned them to bring her right in. A middle-aged woman with a hat that held more feathers than a bird jumped from her seat in the waiting room, stared open-mouthed, then huffed her way out. Jesse didn't miss the distress that crossed Megan's face as she tried to ignore the woman. He would have to ask about her as soon as they saw to Seana.

"Martha." The doctor's bellow echoed off the walls. "Martha, get down here." He acted as if Jesse and Megan weren't even in the room as he went about gathering items he needed. A woman as tall and thin as the doctor rushed into the room. Her hands were busy tying an apron over her gray dress.

"Yes, Myron. What is it now?" Her voice squeaked to a stop as she focused on Seana, who had once more passed into unconsciousness.

The doctor swiveled around from his rummaging. He started

to speak when his gaze caught Megan and Jesse standing by the table where Seana rested. "Oh, this won't do. You'll have to wait outside. I'll let you know when I'm done."

Martha made little shooing noises and motions with her hands, as if she were urging the chickens to leave the pen. Jesse took Megan's arm to lead her from the room. She gave him a panic-stricken look that shot a shaft right through his chest.

"Megan, she's in good hands. The doctor will do the best he can."

Like a sleepwalker, Megan followed in silence. As soon as they cleared the threshold, Martha slammed the door shut. The waiting room, empty now, offered a variety of seats. Jesse chose a ratty sofa and gave Megan's shoulders a gentle push. He sat beside her. She didn't seem to know he was there. Putting his arm around her, he rubbed her shoulder in a soothing motion. With his free hand, he tipped her head until she rested against him. For a few minutes she stayed stiff; then bit by bit, she relaxed. He didn't try to talk, but offered her comfort by his presence. He hoped that would be good enough.

Screams erupted from the other room. Megan jolted upright. Her eyes filled with tears. Jesse caught hold of her. She turned to him.

"I have to go to her."

"You can't."

"She needs me." Megan choked on a sob. "Why can't Momma be here? I can't do this alone."

Jesse hauled her to him, hugging her tight. "Oh, Megan." His whispered words stirred the wisps of hair that had worked free from the braids wrapped around her head. "Since your parents died, you've tried to be both of them to Seana and to yourself. You can't be someone else." He kissed her temple as silent tears slipped down her cheeks. "All God wants is for you to be you and to follow Him. You are so precious to Him, Megan. He didn't allow this as a punishment."

"Then why did He allow my parents and Matt to die?" Megan sounded so much like a little girl that Jesse wanted to pull her onto his lap and snuggle her close.

"I can't answer that." *Lord, please help me here,* Jesse prayed. "I know many of the prophets and people in the Bible asked similar questions about why injustice is allowed. Why do good people die and bad people prosper?"

"And what did God answer?" Megan tilted her head back to look up at him.

Jesse thought of the examples in Scripture for a moment. "Do you remember what he said to Job?" Megan shook her head. He almost forgot what he was supposed to say, at the trusting look in her blue-gray eyes. Jesse cleared his throat and scraped his thoughts together.

"When Job questioned Him, God asked if Job had been present at the beginning of the earth. He asked if Job continued to maintain it."

Megan's brow furrowed.

"You see, Megan, God's ways are so much different than ours that we can't question what He allows or doesn't allow. We have to trust that He will work everything out the right way. God always wants the best for us."

For a moment Megan was silent as she stared at the wall, a faraway look in her eyes. With a sigh, she smiled at Jesse and nodded. "You're right. I've read those verses before. Job suffered much more loss than I have. If he could end up praising God, then who am I to question what's right?" She gave him a watery smile. "That's much easier to say than do."

"You are so right." Jesse grinned.

The office door opened. Dr. Stanhope stepped out and pulled it shut behind him. He finished brushing the sleeves of his shirt down over his arms as he walked toward them. Jesse could feel Megan's tension as she rose to stand next to him. He placed his hand on her elbow to let her know he was there for her.

"The youngster should be fine." Doc smiled, losing his undertaker image. "Those burns are pretty nasty, but Martha will give you some medicine for them and give you instructions for her care. She'll cough for a few days until all the smoke clears out of her lungs. Try to have her drink plenty of liquids to keep her throat from getting too sore."

His brow creased. "She might be in quite a bit of pain for the next few days while the healing starts. I'll give you something to help with that, too."

Jesse breathed a sigh of relief a few minutes later as he helped Megan and Seana settle in the back of the wagon. He planned to get a little something they could eat on the way home and then head out. They should be able to be home in time for the evening chores.

Piling the blankets close to Megan so she could cover up Seana as the weather cooled, he felt her stiffen. He glanced over his shoulder to see Reverend Porter and the banker glaring at them from the sidewalk.

Mr. Sparks rubbed his hands together and gave them a feral smile. "Weather's turning nice, don't you think, Reverend? June will be here before you know it."

thirteen

The extra blanket tucked around Megan's shoulders did nothing to ease the bone-deep chill. She shook, not from the cold as much as from the fear invading every part of her. *God, what are You doing? First, Momma and Papa and Matt. Now Seana's hurt and Mr. Sparks is going to get our farm. Where will I go? What will I do? I have no future.*

From the corner of her eye, she caught a glimpse of Jesse's broad, straight back as he guided the team toward home. Did she even have him? Yes, he'd been wonderful lately, but what about when they lost the farm? What would he do then? Did he truly want to be saddled with her as a wife, or would he continue with his life without a backward thought for her or Seana?

God, there's no one I can turn to. Everyone I know thinks I'm an awful person. Even the preacher in town wouldn't let me into his home. An image of the Bright family popped into her mind. She could feel the weight of the baby in her arms and remember the softness of his skin, the way his round eyes crinkled in laughter as he looked at her. Shame washed over her. God hadn't left her alone. She had no right to question Jesse's allegiance, either. So far, he hadn't given her any reason to believe he would turn his back on her. *Jesus, forgive me. I've been wallowing in self-pity, whining like a little child. Instead, I should be thanking You for saving Seana's life.* With sudden clarity, she could see Jesse throwing himself on top of Seana and rolling to put out the fire. Her throat tightened. If he hadn't been there. . .

"Jesse." His name caught, coming out too soft for him to

hear. She cleared her throat. "Jesse."

He turned and flashed her a smile that made her heart dance. "Getting hungry? The rise where we ate with the Brights is right up ahead. I thought we could stop there and rest a minute while we eat." He glanced at the sun. "We won't be able to stop for long, though. I hope you don't mind."

"That's fine." The words Megan wanted to say wouldn't come out. Jesse turned back around. She watched him lean forward, doing the little that needed doing to guide the team over the rutted road. His hands were strong and capable, yet she knew they could also be gentle. She touched her cheek, recalling the feel of his fingers there. A flood of warmth washed over her at the memory.

Jesus, have I been blind? I've been so caught up in my grief and complaining that I didn't realize You sent Jesse to me, knowing I would need his love and support. Yes, Lord, I do believe he loves Seana and me. I don't know why or how, but he does. Lord, I love him, too. Help me to show him that. Help me be the wife he needs.

"Here we are." The wagon rattled to a stop. Jesse swung down from the seat and held out his arms to help Megan. Seana still slept, so Megan put a blanket under her sister's head and reached out to Jesse. As he lifted her over the side, her breath caught at the feelings flowing through her. The look in his cinnamon eyes held her fast.

When Megan's feet landed, her legs buckled. She would have fallen if Jesse hadn't pulled her against him. She could feel his heart racing almost as fast as hers.

"I guess I sat too long." She tried to laugh, but couldn't.

Jesse's arms tightened. Megan's hand seemed to have a life of its own as her fingers caressed his cheek. The very air around them vibrated with emotion. Megan couldn't breathe. Her small hand slid behind Jesse's head as she tilted her face. Afterwards, she could never be sure who initiated the kiss;

she only knew she didn't want it to end.

"Megan." Jesse's husky whisper told her more than a long discourse. He cupped her cheek with his hand and kissed her until she was breathless. Even then she didn't want to stop. She'd never experienced feelings like this before.

Jesse trailed a line of kisses across her face, then rested his cheek against her forehead. His rapid heartbeat and breathing told her he was as affected by the kisses as she was. *This must be what Momma and Papa felt for each other.* Megan smiled at the memory of her parents' moments of affection, the clear adoration they had for one another.

"We'd better get out our lunch." Jesse stepped back, retrieving the package of sandwiches he'd purchased. Megan checked on Seana, still sound asleep, before walking hand in hand with Jesse up the rise to have their lunch. She felt almost like a shy schoolgirl on a first outing as her husband spread one of the spare blankets on the ground and helped her to sit.

The food was delicious, although Megan wasn't sure what she'd eaten. All her senses seemed to be heightened. She noticed the brush of the breeze against her cheek and smelled the fresh scent of spring in the air. The cushion of dried grass beneath the blanket felt like a feather pillow. Every movement Jesse made, every word he spoke, every smile and look of love in his eyes echoed inside her.

"We'd best be going." Jesse stood and held out his hand to help her up. "I want to be home before dark." After folding the blanket, Megan followed Jesse to the wagon. She didn't want this time to end.

Seana's soft breathing told Megan she still slept. Jesse finished checking the harnesses and helped Megan into the back.

"Wait." Megan placed her hand on his chest. Once more his closeness stole her breath and her thoughts. "I. . ." She glanced again at Seana, then back to Jesse. "Would you mind if I sat up with you for awhile until Seana wakes up?"

Jesse grinned. He slid his hands from her waist to around her back, tugging her close. He gave her a tender, heart-melting kiss. "I wouldn't mind at all." In one swift move, Jesse lifted her to the seat. Megan fussed with her skirts, trying to calm her racing pulse. How could one man be so strong that he could lift someone like her as if she were nothing?

The horses seemed eager to resume the journey. They set off at a good clip, and Megan could almost see pictures of the barn and food in their thoughts. Jesse slipped his arm around her shoulders. She stiffened in surprise for a moment, then relaxed and gave him a shy smile. Leaning her head against his shoulder, she sighed in contentment.

"Why were you passing through here last January, Jesse?"

Silence stretched as he stroked her arm. She felt the light kiss he pressed against her hair. "I was running away."

"From what?"

"From *whom* would be the better question." Jesse paused for so long, she wasn't sure he would answer.

"All my life my father tried to fit me into a mold that wasn't right for me. He wanted me to be a banker just like him and his father before him. Money and status are the two things that matter most to him. We always attended the right functions, with the right people, and wore the right clothes. My parents are well respected."

"Didn't you like banking?"

Jesse shrugged. "I have a different view of life and wealth than my parents or my sisters. Besides, I like being outdoors too much to be cooped up in a building all the time."

"Tell me about your sisters." Megan twisted to look up at him.

"They're both older than me. They married the right men. My father picked them out. Amanda and Patricia both attend the right church and do everything the way Father expected them to. They're perfect—to him."

"He picked out their husbands?" Megan straightened, alarm racing through her. "What about you? Was it Sara?"

Jesse's brow furrowed. "How did you know about Sara?"

"You talked a lot when you were sick. You thought I was Sara." Megan felt heat creeping up her neck to her face. Maybe she shouldn't have said anything.

Sadness settled over Jesse. "Yes, he had Sara picked out several years ago. She was from a family that would be an excellent match, increasing our wealth and holdings." His eyes darkened as if he were begging Megan to understand. "I couldn't marry her. I couldn't spend my life living a lie." He flicked the reins to urge the horses on. "You see, Someone else had a call on my life."

Taking his arm from her shoulders, Jesse wrapped his fingers around Megan's hand, bringing it to his lips for a brief kiss. "I was never like my family. I hated church."

She gave him a startled look. "You hated church?" Megan couldn't help thinking how she dreaded ever going to church again. She'd struggled with separating her feelings about church from her feelings about God.

"The church my family attends is about show. You wear the proper clothes and sit in the designated pew for your status. It's like everything is orchestrated for the congregation's benefit and nothing is there for God." Jesse flicked the reins again. "I didn't realize that until I met Pastor Phillips."

"Who's Pastor Phillips?"

Jesse grinned. "You have to remember you're married to a black sheep. I tended to disappear any chance I got. I'm not sure how it happened, but I found myself in a poorer section of town one day. In looking back, I know God guided me there so I could meet Pastor Phillips." He chuckled. "You would never have guessed the man was a pastor. He was playing a game with some of the neighborhood kids. Even though I dressed differently, they invited me to join them. That was the most fun I'd had in my life.

"From that time on, every chance I got, I slipped off to Pastor Phillips's church. He's the one who taught me who Jesus really is. I had no idea there was more to religion than wearing your best clothes to church once a week."

"Did your parents get angry when they found out where you were going?"

Jesse groaned. "*Angry* doesn't describe them. By the time they found out about Pastor Phillips, I already accepted the call to become a preacher. My father stopped those ideas fast. He even hired a man to follow me to make sure I didn't run with unsavory characters anymore." Jesse stared off into the distance, lost in thought. "He couldn't stop my thoughts, though. I did that all by myself."

"What do you mean?"

He sighed. "I bent to my father's will rather than following God's call."

"You were so young to go against your parents, though." Megan wanted to hug away the hurt she could see in his eyes.

"That's no excuse. Look at all the young men in the Bible who gave up everything to follow God's call: Samuel, David, many of the prophets, the disciples. I was more like Jonah. I ran from what God wanted me to do, and I knew I was running."

Seana moaned. Megan leaned over the seat and placed her fingers on her sister's forehead. Seana quieted. Megan sat back up to find Jesse studying her. She blushed, as thoughts of kissing him again rampaged through her. "Was. . .was banking so awful?"

Jesse gave her a wry smile. "Yes. I hated being cooped up inside that stuffy old building. I loved taking care of the animals and helping the gardener with the plants and grounds." He gazed around at the land spread out before them. "I think God used my willfulness to bring me here. I'm so excited about doing farming as soon as the weather warms up. I found some seed your father had stored in the barn. I thought I'd ride in and buy some more next week so we'll be sure to have enough." He paused.

"I don't know a whole lot about farming. Maybe I'll visit with William Bright and see if he can give me some advice."

"He could help a lot." Megan tried to keep the bitterness from her voice as her fears rose up in a suffocating cloud. "The problem is, why should we go to the trouble to plant the fields when we won't have a farm after June? I don't think we should do Mr. Sparks any favors. He won't take care of the crops."

❧

"Meggie, oww!" Seana began to cry.

Jesse halted the team and grabbed Megan's arm to steady her as she climbed into the wagon bed with Seana. Seana's eyes were wide with fear and pain. She held her body very still, as if simple movements hurt too much to do. Jesse hated the thought of starting the wagon moving, knowing the motion would bring discomfort to the child.

He waited until Megan was settled with Seana's head on her lap. She spoke softly to her sister, calming her down. After a few minutes, Megan looked up at Jesse and nodded. He turned away with the image of her fear and hurt evident in the look she'd given him. More than anything, he wanted to erase those worries; he wanted to see her smile and laugh.

The wagon jounced down the rutted track leading to their farm. No matter which way Jesse guided the team, he could still feel every bump in the road and imagine how those felt like jolts of pain to Seana. With Megan beside her, the young girl was putting up a brave front. She hadn't cried out once since they started off again.

A few minutes later, Seana slept. Megan didn't want to leave her, so they rode in silence. Megan's words came back to Jesse. What about the bank taking back the farm in June? What could he do about that? He had some ideas, and he thought now would be the time to act on them. He'd tried hard to think of some reason Megan's father would have such a large outstanding loan due at an awkward time, but he couldn't come up with anything. He mulled over the information William Bright shared with him and what he knew of banking practices, but nothing made any sense. A gnawing unease deep inside told him something wasn't right here.

He'd gone through Megan's father's papers time and again looking for something about the loan. The only bank papers he'd found showed the loan Mr. Riley took out for seed and equipment three years ago, but there was also documentation that it had been paid off. Had he taken out another loan and not kept the paperwork? That didn't seem to fit with the little he knew about Lee Riley. The man had kept careful records of everything, from what he planted to how the crops produced, valuable information for Jesse or anyone who followed his example. He had a book about the animals and their off-spring. Jesse didn't think very many farmers kept track of things like that, so why did Lee Riley not have anything about a loan that meant he would lose the farm he loved if he didn't pay it off?

The sun was sinking low by the time Jesse drew to a stop in front of the house. His muscles ached as he climbed down. Megan looked as tired as he felt. As his hands circled her waist, he recalled their kisses earlier this afternoon. If only Seana weren't watching them, he would be tempted to steal a few more of those kisses. Megan had no idea how desirable she was, but he intended to show her. He couldn't believe how much he'd grown to love her in the short time he'd known her. She'd become like a precious jewel to him, something of great value that he didn't want to lose.

fourteen

Stepping out of the bedroom, Megan arched her back to ease the ache of weariness. Seana finally slept. Megan didn't know how long this would last. The medicine Doc had given them had lessened the pain enough for sleep to claim her sister.

If only she could take some of the medicine herself. Megan shook her head. The ache inside her was completely different. She knew she would have trouble sleeping tonight because of Jesse and the longing he'd awakened in her. Her cheeks warmed as she recalled his kisses this afternoon. She hadn't wanted him to stop. The way he looked at her, as if she were the most delectable sweet he'd ever seen, made her heart pound and her insides tremble.

Lord, I've fallen in love with him. Is this what You intended when You brought him here? Megan thought back to those first days when she cared for Jesse while he was so sick. Had she even been falling in love with him then? Is that why she hadn't fought marrying him as much as she could have? She knew deep in her heart that she wouldn't have agreed to marry Mr. Sparks that easily. *Jesus, help me to be a good wife to Jesse. Help me encourage him in the calling You've given him.*

A slight movement across the room drew her attention. Jesse squatted in front of the fire. Megan's breath caught in her throat. The firelight flickered and moved like a caress over the planes of Jesse's face, highlighting his toffee-colored hair. His strong hands were still, his eyes staring into the flames as if he were a million miles away. Was he thinking about the girl he didn't marry? Did he have regrets about Sara? Megan didn't want to consider that. She wanted to trust

113

what she'd seen in Jesse's gaze today.

Although she didn't think she'd made a sound, Jesse turned and smiled at her. Megan thought she might melt.

"Would you like me to get you some coffee?" She almost groaned. What a stupid thing to ask. Who would want coffee this late? In fact, why was Jesse still up? He usually went to bed early. She thought he might still be worn down from his bout with pneumonia, but he wouldn't admit to it.

Jesse straightened and brushed at some wood chips on his pants. "I think a glass of warm milk might be better."

"Do you want me to throw it on the fire for you?" Megan slapped her hand over her mouth. She couldn't believe she'd said that.

Tipping his head back, Jesse laughed harder than she'd ever seen him laugh. She couldn't help it, she had to join in. Crossing to the kitchen, Megan hoped their mirth wouldn't wake up Seana.

"I think this fire should stay lit." Jesse gasped, his eyes twinkling. Still chuckling, he strode across the room to join Megan. "I'm glad you can laugh. I was so afraid you'd be beaten down by all that's happened. You're a strong woman, Megan Coulter."

"I only do what I need to do." Megan tried to ignore the rush of excitement that shot through her at his approach.

"I know what I see." Jesse took another step closer. "You're always polite, but you don't give an inch to anything that's wrong. Remember when the reverend tried to make you marry Mr. Sparks?" He grinned. "I think if I hadn't stepped in, Sparks would have been flying—right out the door."

Megan felt her lips twitching. She'd always enjoyed this sort of repartee with her parents, but she'd never been comfortable enough with anyone else to let go and be herself. She chuckled. "Now that would have been a sight to see."

Jesse took another step. She could almost feel the warmth

of his arms as she imagined them around her again. Megan gestured at the stove. "Do you still want some warm milk?" After studying her for a long moment, Jesse nodded.

Within a few minutes, they were seated across the table from each other, sipping the warm drink. Megan had added a little sugar and cinnamon.

"Mmm. This is delicious. What kind of cow gives milk like this?" Jesse's eyes crinkled.

"This is my mother's recipe. We do have sweet grass around here, but nothing with these spices." She met his gaze, then looked away. He made her feel things she'd never felt before. "None of us liked warm milk, so on nights when we couldn't sleep, Momma fixed it this way so we would drink it."

"Did it help you sleep?"

Megan chuckled. "I think sometimes we worked at staying awake just so we could get a sweet treat. Momma and Papa probably knew what we were doing, but they still spoiled us. A lot of parents would have used a switch instead." Megan ran her finger around the rim of her cup. "I hope if I ever have children, I can be half as good a parent."

She jumped as Jesse's warm hand covered hers. "You'll be the best. Look at the way you are with Seana. Anyone who can get along with her sister like you do will make a great mother."

Megan leaned across the table and spoke in a low whisper. "You just haven't seen the times I pinch her when you're not looking."

Jesse grinned. "I may not see them, but I would have heard."

They laughed and Megan straightened. She wondered if she should pull her hand out from under Jesse's and decided not to. His touch felt so right. She wanted more. They should be getting sleep so they'd be ready for tomorrow, but neither one of them seemed eager to end this time together.

Jesse cleared his throat. "Tomorrow I'll ride over to the Brights'."

"That's fine." Megan nodded. "You said you wanted to talk to him about planting. It'll be time soon."

Their conversation wasn't comfortable now, but stilted. The warmth of Jesse's hand covering hers had grown to something more. Megan found herself wishing the table wasn't between them. She wanted him to hold her.

"Do you think Seana will be okay for the night?" Jesse's soft question startled her. His voice sounded funny, almost strained.

Megan nodded. She didn't trust herself to speak. Her mouth felt dry. Jesse stood, never letting go of her hand. He rounded the table, and Megan, too, rose. At his slight tug, she moved toward him as if in a dream. The look of love in his eyes surrounded her, taking away thoughts of anything but her husband.

When he kissed her this time, Megan felt like a princess. She'd given Jesse the opportunity to leave and he hadn't wanted to. He loved her—something she never thought a man would do. She loved him, too, with a deep aching love that she'd never known would be a possibility.

"Megan." Jesse's kisses strayed from her mouth along her jaw. Shivers of delight coursed through her. His arms tightened. The next thing she knew, he swung her up and strode to the bedroom. Her heart thundered loud enough to be heard miles away. Jesse glanced down, a question in his eyes. Megan smiled, her fingers tracing the outline of his face. She barely noticed when he kicked the door shut behind them.

❧

A slight breeze lifted the strands of hair that had worked loose from her braids, sending them dancing across her forehead and cheeks. The fresh scent of spring was in the air. Bright green shoots of grass were poking up from the ground, as if overnight an artist had run his brush across the landscape, adding color to the brown. Megan wanted to throw her arms in the air and twirl in a wild dance of delight that winter was at an end. She settled for taking a deep breath and thanking God for the new life He'd given them.

"Meggie, wait." Seana darted after Megan, her long braids flying behind her. One month had passed since Seana had been burned. Except for the slight pink color on her arms, you couldn't tell where the burns were. Seana scampered up to Megan, her eyes sparkling, her cheeks flushed with excitement. "Meggie, can I go to the creek and play? I finished the chores you gave me. Please?"

"You know you can't go to the creek by yourself. Especially this time of year, when we've had so much rain." Megan stretched out her hand to Seana. Her sister's health had been improving as winter faded. As she felt stronger, Seana had also been showing some rebellion. Megan thought Seana missed their parents more than she would let on, but she hadn't been able to get Seana to admit that.

"I'm old enough to go there. Matt could go by himself." Seana put her hands on her hips. "I know how to swim if I fall in. I only want to see if I can find some frog eggs. Matt showed me how."

"Matt was a lot older than you. When he was your age, he couldn't go to the creek by himself, either." A lump wedged in Megan's throat. Matt had always taken Seana with him on his jaunts to fish or hunt for tadpoles and frogs. Their age difference didn't seem to matter. Matt doted on his younger sister.

"Why don't you come with me? I'm taking some water and a piece of corn bread out to Jesse."

"Why?"

"He's been working hard, and supper is still three hours away." Megan studied Seana's defiant stance. "Don't you think he deserves a little something? Remember how Momma used to do this for Papa?"

"Jesse isn't my papa." Seana hurled the words like stones.

Megan flinched. Seana whirled and ran back to the house, but not before Megan could see the tears brimming in her eyes.

Jesus, I don't know what to do here. She's hurting so bad. Do I just wait, or do I punish her for insolence? I'm not a parent, Lord. Help me.

The joy seemed to have gone from the day as she trudged on to the field where Jesse plowed the soil. Megan attempted to erase the concern from her face, pasting on a smile when Jesse waved at her, then strode in her direction, leaving the team to rest.

"Hey, Beautiful. This is a pleasant surprise." Jesse brushed a sweet kiss across her lips.

"It is not a surprise." Megan couldn't help the giggle that escaped. "I do this every day."

Taking a long drink of water, Jesse winked at her. "Maybe the surprise isn't seeing you, but realizing how much more I love you every day."

Megan waved her hand in front of her face. "Whew, it's getting hot out here. It must be all the blarney floating around."

Jesse laughed and drew her close for another kiss. "That was the honest truth, even if you don't believe it." He released her. "Now why don't you give me that piece of corn bread before it's completely squashed and tell me what has you so upset."

Megan glanced down at what had once been a beautiful square of corn bread, but now looked more like something the horse stepped on. She flushed and handed the flattened piece to Jesse. "I'm sorry."

"You're avoiding the real issue." Jesse undid the cloth covering and took a huge bite. He didn't seem to care about the shape of his food.

Megan sighed and glanced back toward the house. "It's Seana again. I don't know what to do, Jesse. She's so moody lately. I thought she would have been rebellious over losing her parents months ago. Instead, she acts like they died yesterday."

Jesse took another long drink of water. "Hey." He pulled her close. Megan rested her head against his chest, listening to the steady thump of his heart. "She's been sick and hurt, Megan. I don't think she felt well enough to understand the loss. Give her time, Angel. She'll come around."

"But she resents your being here."

"That's natural, I think. She sees me as trying to take her father's place. Maybe in her child's mind, she wonders if she gets rid of me, maybe they'll be able to come back." He gave her a tight hug, then handed her the water container. "I'll try to quit a little early tonight. Maybe I can take her to the creek and do some fishing. Fresh fish for supper might be a nice change."

"Okay." Megan sniffed and wiped her nose. She gave Jesse a sly smile. "If she pushes you in, can you swim?"

"Nope, you'll have to come along and rescue me." He gave her a quick kiss and headed back to the horses. "I'll stop in about an hour. Don't say anything to her. She might think of an excuse not to go."

&

His hair still wet from washing up, Jesse whistled as he opened the door to the house. Seana sulked in the corner while Megan chopped something for supper. The tension in the room could stop a train.

"Seana, I need some help." Jesse didn't glance at Megan, not wanting to give their conspiracy away.

"I'm busy." Seana grabbed up her doll, pretending to do something important with the toy.

"You can bring Ennis with you." Jesse paused to frown and rub his chin as if in deep thought. "The problem is she might get dirty and wet." He shrugged. "Oh well, I'm sure you can clean her up."

"What do you need me to do?" Seana was trying hard not to be interested.

Jesse sighed. "Well, there's some fish down in the creek, hollering to be caught. I hoped to find someone who could show me the best place to dig up worms and maybe even the best fishing holes."

Seana stared down, silent and still. Jesse turned to Megan. "Will you go with me, Megan? I really don't know where to go, and I'm hungry for a mess of fresh fish. I've been thinking about that all afternoon."

Megan opened her mouth to answer when Seana jumped to her feet. "She doesn't know. She never wanted to go fishing. Only Matt and me did that."

Jesse swung back around to face Seana. "Well, if you won't help me out, then Megan's the only hope I have. Will you help me?"

Seana shot a look at Megan that might have been triumph. "Come on, I know the best spots. Matt showed me all of them."

"Do we have some fishing poles?"

"They're out in the shed." A seed of excitement shone in Seana's eyes. "There's a can for worms out there, too."

"Why don't you go look for them while I instruct your sister on the fine art of getting ready to cook fish?" Jesse winked at Seana. She did her best to wink back, then darted out the door.

He heard the sniffle before he turned around. Megan wiped at her eyes with a corner of her apron. "Thank you."

"Thank me for what?" He went to her and wrapped his arms around her. He arched his brow. "Say, have you been chopping onions? You seem to be crying."

Stretching up, Megan dragged his head down and gave him a kiss. Jesse kissed her back. "I'd better go before I forget what I'm doing."

"Aren't you going to instruct me in the fine art of cooking fish?" Megan's gaze was wide and innocent.

He chuckled and kissed her again. When she was breathless, he stepped back. "Those were my instructions. Now you have to figure them out." Laughing, Jesse headed for the door. "We'll be back in an hour, Angel." He winked. "If you hear me hollering, come to my rescue."

fifteen

"I give up." Jesse sank down on the bank of the creek. "There aren't any worms to be found here. The only way to catch a fish is to try to grab one out of the water, and I'm no good at that, either."

"Matt did that once." Seana perched on a rock near the creek, her arms crossed, her back rigid. She'd been bouncing and excited until they stood on the small hill leading down to the winding stream. She froze, and Jesse could almost see the memories of fun times spent with her brother parading through her mind. He'd tried everything he could think of to reach her, but nothing worked. Acting as if he couldn't do this was his last resort.

"I've heard of people being able to do that, but not when the water is so cold."

Seana's chin tilted up a notch. "Matt did it in the summer. If it was warmer, I could show you how."

"Did you catch fish with your hands, too?"

She shook her head. "No, but I watched how Matt did it."

Jesse could see the sheen of tears in her eyes. "Me, I have to have a fat, juicy worm, or I can't catch a thing." Jesse plucked a blade of grass, taller down here by the water, and stuck it in his mouth. "Of course, I didn't have much chance to fish in the city."

"Matt said city folk don't know nothing about living."

"Matt could be right." Jesse's thoughts strayed to the values embraced by the people he knew. How many of them were miserable trying to keep up with fashion, wealth, and the status of their neighbors? They didn't have any idea how precious life could be until too late.

"Why don't you go back to the city?"

Jesse stilled. He'd almost missed the words, they were so quiet. *Lord, what do I say?* He studied the set of Seana's shoulders and thought of all she'd lost since he'd arrived. How could he have been so insensitive? She needed love and understanding—attention. That's why she was lashing out.

"Seana, I don't want to take Matt's place or your papa's."

"Then why did you come here?" Her chin trembled.

"Because this is where the Lord brought me. I was lost in the storm. He led me to you."

"Why?"

Jesse sat up. "Maybe because I needed your help. Maybe because you needed mine, too."

"I don't need you. I need Papa and Matt and Momma. They can take care of me just fine. I want them." She bent her knees and wrapped her arms around them, huddled in a ball. "Megan doesn't want you, either."

"I don't believe that's true, Seana. Have you talked to Megan about this?"

Seana shook her head and swiped the tears from her face. "It's true, I know. We don't want you here."

"If I leave, who will plow and plant the fields for you?"

"I can do it." Seana gave him a fierce look. "I've watched Papa."

Jesse quirked one eyebrow. "You can hitch a team to the plow? Have you ever done that?"

"No, but Momma always says there's a first time for everything. I know I can do it."

"Okay, I'll make you a deal." Jesse waited as Seana narrowed her gaze a moment before nodding. "You help me find a worm and catch a couple of fish for supper, and tomorrow I'll let you help me do the plowing."

He tried not to hold his breath or look anxious as she considered his offer. Seana jumped down from the rock and walked over to him. "Deal." She held out her hand. "Then when you see how good I am, you'll leave, right?"

"Fair enough." Jesse nodded. "But only if Megan wants me to go. She has a say in this, too."

They shook hands, and Seana walked to the edge of the creek bank. Taking a stick, she pried a rock loose and dug in the soil for a minute. With a grunt of triumph, she slipped a couple of fat worms free from the dirt, holding them aloft for his inspection. Jesse prayed he'd done the right thing. He wanted to reach Seana and help her through her hurt.

Threading a worm onto his hook, Jesse followed Seana downstream. She pointed to a spot in the creek, and he landed his bait there on the second try. The water swirled and eddied around the rocks and brush, the sound as soothing as a mother's crooning to her infant. He settled back against a tree, the rough bark poking through his shirt. Seana sat on a rock, her gaze glued to the spot where his line dipped below the surface of the stream.

Within minutes Jesse felt a hard tug on the pole. He sat up, his gaze going to Seana. She leaned forward, an excited expression making her look like the child she was. Jesse fought back a grin and began to work the fish to the edge of the water, where he could flip it up on the bank.

A squeal escaped Seana as she pounced on the flopping fish. For the moment, she seemed to have forgotten her dislike of Jesse. He could see her having done this many times in the past with Matt. She held the trout as high as she could.

"Bring him over here." Jesse pointed to a spot away from the creek in case the fish wiggled loose from the hook. He'd had many fish flop right back into the water before he could grab them.

Putting a new worm on the hook, Jesse ignored the wriggling fish and looked at Seana. "Do you think we can catch another one in this spot?"

She frowned at the swirling water, then nodded.

"All right. You toss the worm in, and I'll work on cleaning

this fish while you catch the next one." He tried to act nonchalant about the proposal, but didn't miss the widening of Seana's eyes as she glanced from him to the worm dangling from the hook to the stream. It took her several tries and a little assistance to land the bait in the right spot, but Jesse couldn't help the satisfied feeling that welled up inside as he went a little way downstream to clean the first fish.

"Jesse, I got one." Seana's voice squeaked. Jesse crashed through the brush just in time to see her flip a trout onto the bank.

"This one is even bigger than the one I caught." Jesse placed his cleaned fish alongside hers. "I think you beat mine by at least two inches."

Seana clapped her hands. Jesse was amazed that the sulky girl of a few minutes ago could be so changed. Maybe her anger would pass as she learned he wasn't trying to replace her family—or the cause of them being gone. Jesse determined he would have to win the girl over. She deserved loving, and God sent him here for a purpose.

They caught two more fish before Jesse declared they had plenty for supper. Both of Seana's fish were bigger than Jesse's. She skipped ahead of him all the way back to the house. The sun hung low in the west. Chores needed doing before supper, so Jesse sent Seana to the house with the catch while he headed for the barn. Although tired, he worked fast. He couldn't wait to eat some fresh trout. Plus, the thought of seeing Megan again made the chores a breeze.

&

"Meggie, look." Seana rushed through the door, a string of fish in one hand, poles in the other.

Megan shut the oven door and set the pan of biscuits out to cool. "Those are nice, Seana." She left the kitchen to admire them.

"I caught two of them all by myself. These two." Seana pointed out the two biggest trout. "Jesse couldn't even figure out how to find worms. I had to show him where they are and then show him the best spots to fish."

"Sounds like without you we might not have had any supper tonight." Megan bit back the urge to caution her sister not to brag. Right now Seana needed encouraging, not discouraging. "Why don't you wash up? You can help me with supper. We should try to have everything ready when Jesse gets in from doing the chores."

Seana's face clouded over. Her lower lip stuck out a bit. "All you ever think about anymore is Jesse. You don't care about me. You don't even miss Momma, Papa, and Matt." She threw the fish on the table. "Well, I hate him." Seana rushed to her bedroom, leaving Megan stunned and in tears.

Her hands shaking, Megan picked up the stringer and carried it to the basin of water she had prepared to wash the fish. It wouldn't hurt them to soak for a little while so she could take care of this matter. Taking a deep breath, she headed for Seana's room, wishing that she could take with her some of her mother's wisdom in handling these matters. This was going too far and needed to be addressed.

"Seana?" Megan stepped into the bedroom. Her sister huddled on the bed, rolled into a ball. Her shoes, still damp from being near the creek, dripped pieces of dried grass on the bed and floor. "Seana, take off those shoes. You know better than to have them on the furniture."

"You're not my momma." Seana's voice was so muffled, Megan wondered if she'd heard right.

Taking a deep breath, Megan tried to count. She shouldn't have begun this conversation by pointing out her sister's faults. Her mother and father both told her she was too bossy with her sister and brother. Closing her eyes, she tried to think of how her mother would have handled this. "What did Momma say right before she left for town?"

A sob racked Seana's thin frame. "She said you were in charge while they were gone."

"That's right, Seana. I'm still in charge."

"I don't want you to be. I want Momma and Papa."

The bed rustled as Megan sat down beside her sister. "I don't want to be in charge any more than you want me to be. I want Momma and Papa and Matt home, too." She smoothed Seana's hair away from her tear-streaked face. "The problem is, they won't be coming home. We have to be brave and live like they want us to. Do you think they would be happy to see you acting like this?"

A hiccupping sob shook Seana. "No." She flung herself at Megan. "Meggie, it's his fault. I know it."

"What? Whose fault?"

"Jesse's." Seana's eyes met Megan's. Megan could see her sister pleading for understanding.

"You think our family died because of Jesse?"

Seana nodded.

"Why would you think that?"

"Because he came here the day they died. It's his fault."

Megan hugged her sister close, aching inside for the loss that was just now catching up to the young girl. She'd had trouble dealing with this, too, but all along she'd assumed Seana was too young to understand death. Her assumption that Seana would go right on despite missing their parents and brother had been wrong. What should she do now?

"Jesse was lost in the storm. He nearly died before I found him. How could he have done any harm to our family?"

"I don't know, but he did." Seana shook with sobs. Megan began to rock her, hoping to ease the girl's pain.

"Seana, you're looking for someone to blame for their deaths, but there isn't anyone. Sometimes things like this happen. Death can come to us all—it will, in fact. We have to be ready to accept that even when it hurts."

"I want them back." Seana pushed free. "You have to say those things because you married Jesse."

Weariness settled over Megan. She didn't know what to do.

She had no idea what Momma and Papa would have done. "I have to fix supper. You stay in here. Take off those muddy shoes. Think about what you've said. Jesse has done nothing but be kind to us since he's been here. He doesn't deserve your nastiness."

Megan's legs trembled as she walked from the room. Her stomach tensed with the feeling that she'd failed her parents when they left her in charge. Her earlier question to Seana now haunted her. What would her parents say about how she was doing?

She didn't hear anything from Seana as she prepared the fish for cooking. By the time Jesse came through the door, the smell of supper permeated the air. Megan's stomach rumbled. They hadn't had fresh trout in months.

"Oh, that smells so good." Jesse drew in a deep breath, his face split in a wide grin. After hanging his hat on a hook near the door, he clumped into the kitchen and swept Megan into his arms. She couldn't get over how affectionate her husband was. She loved the attention he lavished on her. Whenever she approached him, he gave her his immediate consideration, no matter what else he was doing.

"How's the most beautiful girl in a hundred miles?" Jesse nuzzled her neck, sweeping kisses up to her cheek.

"You are going to be eating burned fish if you keep this up." Megan tried to sound fierce, but her giggles spoiled the effect.

"I'll catch more," Jesse murmured against her ear. "You taste better than any old fish, anyway."

"Jesse." Megan slapped at his shoulder. He grinned and landed a kiss on her lips. She quit fighting, even if she hadn't been protesting in earnest. His kisses were so sweet. She couldn't seem to get enough.

"Stop that. You're killing her, too." Seana's scream from across the room jerked Megan and Jesse apart. Megan blinked and stared at her sister, whose face had turned red with rage.

"Seana, we were kissing."

"No, he was gonna kill you like he did them."

Anger coursed through Megan. "Jesse did not kill anyone, Seana. You've seen Momma and Papa kissing like that. What's wrong with you?"

"I hate him." Seana clutched her doll tight to her chest. Her eyes shone bright with unshed tears. She looked like a forlorn waif, but her emotions were coming out as hatred toward Jesse. Megan knew they couldn't allow that to continue.

"Seana, that's enough. I want you to apologize to Jesse."

"I won't."

"Do you remember what Momma would do when you behaved like this?"

Seana stared at her for a moment. The fight seemed to trickle out of her until she hung her head. "She whipped me with a switch."

"That's right." Megan's heart was breaking as she tried to remain firm. "Jesse is my husband, your brother-in-law. I was wrong earlier when I told you I was in charge. Jesse is the one in charge here, just like Papa was the head of the house before." Megan waited a moment to let that sink in. "You will treat Jesse with respect."

Her tone softened. "I know you're missing our family. I am, too. But you can't blame Jesse for something he didn't do. All right?"

"Yes." Seana's braids shivered as she nodded her head.

"Now get ready for supper." Megan forced a light tone, hoping to ease the tension. "The fish you caught are almost ready for you to eat them."

Seana shuffled back to her room to put up her doll. Megan could see the glint of moisture in Jesse's eyes. He looked so gruff sometimes because of his size, but he had a tender heart.

"She wants me to leave." Jesse's voice told the hurt he felt. He tried to smile, but failed. "At the creek she told me you don't want me to stay anymore."

sixteen

The evening air carried a chill, making Megan glad she'd brought a shawl with her when Jesse suggested they take a walk. Her whole body cried out with exhaustion from the tension of the evening. Seana had calmed down, but they all still felt her rejection of Jesse. Now her sister slept, and Jesse walked silently by Megan's side. She could almost feel his hurt and frustration.

"I'm so sorry about what Seana said."

Jesse squeezed her hand. "She's a child. I'm sure she'll be okay in time." They walked in silence for a few minutes.

"I should have seen this coming." Megan fought to speak around the lump in her throat. "She cried when my parents and Matt were gone, but it's slowly sinking into her that they're gone for good. She always did want Momma to hold her for hours when she was sick."

Stars twinkled across the expanse of the sky. On the horizon, the moon was just peeking above the hills. Megan felt choked by the responsibility weighing down on her. She felt guilty over her anger at her parents for leaving her with this mess. What kind of daughter was she to feel this way?

"I don't know what to do." The words came out on a sob.

Jesse halted, pulling her close. "Seana's gone through a lot, Megan. Give her time. She's also a Christian now. You can use Bible verses to guide her. I'll be there to help, but she already resents me. I don't want to turn her away completely."

Her head rested against his broad chest, and she closed her eyes. The steady beat of his heart calmed her. "You're better than warm milk."

"What?" Jesse tipped her head back and smiled down at her.

Megan could feel the heat warming her face. "I meant. . . when you hold me." She struggled to find the right words. "When you hold me like this, I forget all about my troubles. You make me relax. I feel so content."

He chuckled and let her lean against him again. "I could say the same for you. You know, I really thought I'd never get married, but now I can't imagine life without you." The kiss that followed stole her breath. The next one made her forget everything.

Jesse broke the kiss and stepped back, his breathing ragged. He caught hold of her hand. "I brought you out here to talk. If we don't start walking again, I'm going to forget what I had to say and just suggest we return to the house." He paused, then stepped closer. "Come to think of it, maybe we can talk tomorrow."

"Oh, no you don't." Megan gave a breathless laugh and swatted at him. "You can't tell me you have something important to talk about, then put it off. I won't be able to sleep."

"Maybe I was just wanting to get you out here where we could be alone."

Megan tilted her head and tried to hide a smile. "That won't work. We were alone in the house, since Seana sleeps like a bear in hibernation."

"Perhaps I wanted to be romantic." Jesse gestured up at the millions of stars. He drew her close and lowered his lips toward hers.

"Won't work." As she murmured the words, she sighed with longing. She didn't know if she wanted to continue with this intimacy or hear what he had to say.

"You're right." Jesse held her tight for a few minutes. "I need to talk to you about this."

Megan waited, content to remain in his embrace forever. She couldn't imagine what would be so important. They'd already discussed Seana, the plowing was underway, and Jesse had visited with William Bright a couple of times for advice on managing the farm.

He cleared his throat. Stepping back, he took her hand and began to walk. "The other day when I was at the Brights', William and I got into a discussion about church and religion."

Megan tensed, but remained silent, waiting to see what Jesse had to say.

"William and Edith haven't been back to church since the last day we were there. Reverend Porter did come to visit them." Jesse squeezed her hand as she tried to pull away. He wouldn't let go.

"Porter spouted some religious jargon, trying to convince them that he was in the right that day. They didn't fall for it. In fact, William told Porter to leave and never come back when he started telling them all the rumors about your reputation being sullied."

Anger made Megan feel taut as a strung bow. She wanted to say something in her defense, but knew there was nothing to say. Her hand began to ache, and she realized how tightly she had gripped Jesse's fingers. She made herself relax the hold she had on him.

"I didn't say this to make you mad or to bring up hurtful things." Jesse sounded anxious that she understand. Looking up into his dark eyes, Megan attempted a smile, but failed.

"William and Edith both miss the fellowship with other believers."

"Then they need to go back to church. They shouldn't stay away on my account."

"They aren't, Angel." Jesse embraced her. "William says they won't go back to a church where the reverend spreads gossip and treats the parishioners like you were treated."

"There aren't any other churches close enough to attend." Megan thought about how much she missed church functions.

Even though she didn't care to be around people a lot, she still liked hearing the Word of God preached to a group of believers and nonbelievers. She wanted to feel a part of God's family.

Jesse took a deep breath. "That's what I wanted to talk to you about. We've discussed the idea of starting a church a few times, but haven't done anything yet." He hesitated as if gathering his thoughts. "I invited the Brights to come over on Sunday and worship with us." He stopped, turning her to face him. Megan had to fight a smile at the hopeful look he gave her. He reminded her of Matt as a little boy, begging to do something he wasn't sure would be allowed.

"That is the best idea I've heard in a long time." Megan's excitement began to grow. "Edith will probably bring something, and we can share a meal after the service. I can't wait." She hugged Jesse. "I don't know why you were so worried. The Brights are good friends. We don't get to see each other often. I'm always happy to have them visit, and worshiping together will be even better."

Pushing her back a step, Jesse took hold of her hands. "That's not quite all." She quieted as he paused. "William wants to invite some of the others who live within traveling distance of our place. Most of them live too far to get to Yankton, but they could come here on a Sunday."

Fear gripped Megan. She closed her eyes. Having close friends over to worship with was one thing. Having a crowd was another. Who knew what someo.. .ight have heard? Then more rumors would be spread, and she would be the target of those looks and comments that hurt more than any physical pain she'd ever experienced.

"Megan, look at me." He waited until she opened her eyes. "You have nothing to be ashamed of. There are always people who will gossip. That's why gossip is mentioned right alongside of murder in the Bible." He pulled her into his embrace.

"Don't let your fears hinder what we should do for Jesus. I've promised Him to serve wherever and however He wants. I thought that meant going somewhere far away." She leaned back to gaze up at him. He kissed her and gave her a reassuring smile. "Now I understand He wants me right here. That's one of the reasons I'm here, or God is using me here, despite my willfulness. There's a need for a church and I'd like to start one. Will you help me?"

Megan leaned her forehead against Jesse's chest. He was so strong and sturdy and tender. She loved him so much. Could she stand with him? Would God give her the strength and courage to do so?

For the first time, Megan realized how much she depended on her parents' faith. Although she'd always believed, she never had to stand on her own before. She could almost feel God ask, "Whom will you serve this day?" Lifting her head, she met Jesse's gaze as tears filled her eyes.

"Whatever God wants you to do, I'll be right there."

"Thank you." Jesse whispered the words as he leaned close for a long kiss. By the time the kiss ended, they were both breathless again. "Now, I think it's time for the two of us to go back home, don't you?" His eyes twinkled with love and excitement. Megan knew her eyes must reflect those same feelings.

๛

The yard held a scattering of makeshift tables on one side. The other side was lined with benches waiting for the neighbors to arrive for their first church service. Jesse yanked at the collar of his shirt and tried to pray harder. He'd never led a complete service before, although he'd helped Pastor Phillips several times. Megan assured him the people would love his preaching, but he still had the tingling of nerves letting him know he was depending too much on himself and not enough on God.

A wagon rattled into sight. William and Edith waved, their boys and Sally jumping down almost before the wagon had a chance to stop. Seana, delighted at the chance to spend the day with her friend, dashed from the house. Every day, Seana made several trips to the barn to see if Shadow or Mama Kitty had their babies yet. Now she grabbed Sally's hand and dragged her in that direction, most likely hoping to have kittens to show her.

"Mornin', William." Jesse greeted the man he'd come to think of as a friend. William was steady, a hard worker, and willing to give advice, not ridicule, to a newcomer.

"Mornin', Jesse." William took the baby and helped Edith to the ground. "There are two more wagons behind us. I think it's Harry Price and Joseph Martin, with their families. Caleb Duncan promised they'd come, too." William gave a slow grin. "With their fourteen young 'uns, they'll about fill up the benches."

Jesse shook his head. Fourteen. That was a passel of children, for sure. "Once we have the service, we can take the benches to the tables while the women set out the food." Jesse slapped William on the back. "Thanks for all the help yesterday. I couldn't have gotten ready without you."

William studied the makeshift tables and benches thrown together from scraps. Jesse knew he was thinking of the work they'd put in, when William showed up unexpectedly with a wagon full of scrap lumber, a hammer, and some nails. He wanted this church to work out as much as Jesse did.

"I've been praying for years that God would send us someone who could preach a good Bible-based message and who would be willing to meet with folks who couldn't make the drive to Yankton." William stared off in the distance, not meeting Jesse's gaze. "You're an answer to prayer."

"I don't know. You haven't heard me preach yet." He watched as another wagon came into view.

William turned and lowered his voice, although no one else was near. "Before the others arrive, I wanted to ask if you'd heard anything back from the letters you sent."

"I haven't been to town to check the mail. I should be going this week sometime to get supplies. If I hear anything, I'll be over and let you know." Jesse stepped forward with William to greet the new family driving into the yard. He hadn't told Megan that Mr. Sparks had stopped by William's place, offering to buy it from him. Sparks told William if he didn't sell, they would be neighbors soon when he took over the Riley place. The man refused to think of it as the Coulter place. He wouldn't even acknowledge Jesse when they passed on the street in Yankton.

Another wagon clattered to a stop. Jesse busied himself unhitching horses and directing the older boys to where the stock could be watered and penned up for the day. Women called greetings to one another as they herded toddlers and carried food to the house. The older children squealed in delight as they played a game of tag to pass the time until everyone arrived. The peace and quiet that usually filled Jesse's day turned to chaos, but he didn't mind a bit. The Holy Spirit had given him a message for these people, and now that the time had come, he couldn't wait to share God's Word with them. As he watched the chatter and joy these people who lived in isolation exhibited as they met with one another, Jesse felt a welling up of love and compassion. For the first time, he began to understand what Pastor Phillips meant when he talked about loving his flock. With God's help, these people would become Jesse's flock of believers.

In no time the horses were cared for, the food put in the house, the children gathered, and everyone seated on the rough benches, waiting for Jesse to begin. He looked out at their eager, expectant faces and thrilled to the work God had prepared for him to do.

"Good morning. Thank you all for coming." Jesse cleared his throat and glanced at Megan. He'd been afraid she would be uncomfortable with the gathering, but with Edith arriving first, Megan had relaxed and seemed to be enjoying the company.

"Pastor Dan Phillips taught me most of what I know of the Bible. I enjoyed many of his services and would like to pattern this one after some of his." He grinned. "That means I'd like to start off with some singing, and I'm looking for one of the men here to volunteer to lead the songs."

The men glanced at one another from the corners of their eyes, looking as if they'd rather be a hundred miles away than here. Jesse had no idea who to call on because he didn't know anyone other than William well enough to elect them. William admittedly had trouble carrying a tune in a bucket.

"Caleb's oldest boy, Samuel, has a fine voice. I've heard him singing in the fields." William pointed to the boy in question. The youth's face turned bright pink, and he ducked his head.

"Samuel." Jesse waited until the boy looked up at him. His bright eyes held a mixture of longing and embarrassment. "Would you like to come and help me with the singing this first time? Then, if you like, you can take over the other Sundays."

With Samuel's help, they sang several verses of "Amazing Grace" and "Rock of Ages." Without an instrument to guide them, they were probably a little off-key, but Jesse didn't mind, and he knew God didn't care, either. These people were having a great time worshiping together.

"Before you sit down, Samuel, I'd like to do one more song. Do any of you know 'The Church's One Foundation'? "

Samuel frowned and shook his head, as did the others. Jesse nodded, knowing they might not have heard the song yet. "I'd like to teach this one to you because, as we begin a church here, I want us to remember who the founder of our church is. I'll sing through the first verse to show you how it goes. Then you can join me the second time."

> *The Church's one foundation is Jesus Christ her Lord;*
> *She is His new creation by water and the word.*
> *From heaven He came and sought her to be His holy*
> *   bride;*
> *With His own blood He bought her and for her life*
> *   He died.*

By the time the people finished singing, there wasn't a dry eye in the crowd. Blessed by how they longed to worship, Jesse hoped he would be able to deliver the message God had given him for these believers.

seventeen

Throughout the singing and introductory statements he gave, Megan couldn't take her eyes off Jesse. She forgot her discomfort with the crowd of people. She forgot her concern about Seana. Some change had transformed Jesse into a confident leader. She'd never seen that side of him before. His very demeanor took her breath away, and his words put a longing in her heart to know Jesus better.

"I'd like to read a portion of one of the psalms. Those who have their Bibles can follow along." Jesse held his Bible in one hand while he flipped through the pages. "I'll be reading from Psalm 90, verses 14 through 17. 'O satisfy us early with thy mercy; that we may rejoice and be glad all our days. Make us glad according to the days wherein thou hast afflicted us, and the years wherein we have seen evil. Let thy work appear unto thy servants, and thy glory unto their children. And let the beauty of the Lord our God be upon us: and establish thou the work of our hands upon us; yea, the work of our hands establish thou it.'"

Closing his eyes, Jesse prayed a simple prayer, then studied the people who waited in silence for him to begin. For some reason Megan could feel something different about this morning. Many Sundays Jesse shared Scripture with her and Seana. He'd taught her a lot, but today felt different somehow. She sensed a presence that hadn't been here, or at least as noticeable, before.

"Those four verses hold a wealth of wisdom I could talk about." Jesse stood tall, the slight breeze ruffling his hair. "I could talk about being satisfied with God's mercy or rejoicing and being glad all our days. I want to speak to you instead about the years wherein we have seen evil and the choices we have to make because of that."

Silence fell heavy over the group. This wasn't what Megan expected for a first service. She leaned forward to hear what he would say next.

"We've all experienced hard times: crop failures, disease, loss of loved ones. How many of us are able to walk away from tragedies without anger or frustration? How many of us are glad that those things happened?" A murmur rumbled through the group. Jesse waited a moment for it to die down.

"Look again at verse fifteen. Moses is the writer of this psalm. We all know Moses suffered a lot in his life. He didn't have an easy time, but here he is asking God to make him glad that he's been afflicted. Why is that? Take a minute and think about some difficult time you've gone through. Have you been able to thank God for that trial? Are you glad you experienced it?"

The breath seemed to drain from Megan's body. She thought of the deaths of her family, the lies spread about her both back East and out here. How could she be glad any of that happened? God couldn't expect that.

Jesse's tone softened. "That's hard to do. I believe it's only through God's grace and the working of the Holy Spirit that we're able to be glad in such circumstances. Why should we do this? Look at verses sixteen and seventeen."

Glancing down at her Bible, Megan drew in a sharp breath. Her heart pounded. The hairs on her arms stood up. She tingled as if a presence surrounded her. She listened as Jesse spoke, knowing his words speaking to her heart were a message from God to her. The fact that God chose to speak to her in any form or fashion made her want to weep. He loved her. It didn't matter what happened to her then or now, God loved her. He sent Jesse to be her husband because He loved her.

Jesus would give her the courage to be right for Jesse, to encourage him in all that God had planned for him to do.

"When we choose to be glad for the afflictions God allows in our life, we will see the glory of God every day." Several heads nodded as Jesse continued. "Do you want to be beautiful? Then be glad at what the Lord's done in your life. Let Him establish the work of your hands and all you do will hold His beauty."

Jesse shut his Bible and looked at each person. "God has called me to preach His Word—to be a pastor. I'd like to be your pastor. I would like for the Lord to establish a work for me here in this community for those who aren't able to travel farther." He smiled at Megan. "My wife and I invite all of you to come every Sunday and hear the Word of God preached. You're all welcome to worship with us every week."

They were dismissed after William led them in prayer. The men moved to shake hands with Jesse and carry the benches to the tables, while the women rushed inside to set out the food. Megan lost count of the number of people who told her how much they appreciated the service and how they looked forward to next Sunday. Seana and her friends raced around the yard like young colts finally free from a pen. Megan couldn't seem to stop smiling. She hadn't had the chance to speak with Jesse, but every time he looked at her, it was like a physical touch of reassurance and love.

❧

"Did you ever wish for a smooth road without any ruts?" Jesse grinned at Megan as the wagon rocked through another pothole. With the recent rains, the road to town had grown increasingly more difficult to navigate. Sometimes Jesse feared they would break a wheel in the places he couldn't avoid.

"Do they have streets like that in Chicago? I can't remember such luxuries." Megan smiled up at him, her cheeks flushed with a healthy glow. Her eyes sparkled. Jesse wanted nothing more than to stop the wagon, hold her, and kiss her.

"Would you please stop that?" He guided the team around another hole.

"Stop what?"

"Stop looking so beautiful. We'll be late getting to town and late getting home, if you don't."

"How will my looking at you a certain way make us late?" Megan gave him an incredulous look.

"Because I might do this." Jesse pulled on the reins and stopped the horses. Taking Megan in his arms, he kissed her with all the desire he felt.

"Ick. I can't look." Seana made sounds from the back of the wagon like she was going to be sick. Jesse chuckled and released Megan, whose cheeks were even more flushed now.

Megan fanned her face with her hand. "Seana, you should pray for a wonderful husband like Jesse."

"Not if he makes me sick like you've been."

"You've been sick?" Jesse studied his wife's healthy glow. He'd never seen her look so good.

Megan shrugged. "I've been sick a couple of mornings this week. Certain smells seem to be upsetting my stomach." She smiled and raised her voice so Seana could hear. "The sickness has nothing to do with Jesse."

"Tess Duncan says it does." Seana crossed her arms, looking defiant. Her attitude toward him had improved, but Jesse knew they still had a ways to go before she would want him around for good.

"Why does Tess think Jesse is making me sick?" Megan's eyes twinkled with mirth.

"Tess told me her mother says her father is the reason for some of her sickness. Her mother gets sick to her stomach and tired, then she gets fat, and then they have another baby in the house."

Jesse felt the breath whoosh out of him. Megan's eyes

widened. He could see that she was considering if it were true. He sat perfectly still, watching the play of emotions across her face. When her eyes began to glitter and her hand covered her lips as they formed an *O* of wonder, Jesse knew. Megan's hand strayed to touch her abdomen. Jesse couldn't resist covering her hand with his, as awe filled him at the thought that they would have a child. In a few months, he, Jesse Coulter, would be a father.

"Is it true?" At his whispered question, Megan looked up. Her eyes shone.

"I think it is." She sounded shocked and delighted at the same time. "I hadn't considered this as the reason I was getting sick. It hasn't been bad. Edith was so sick, she couldn't get out of bed."

"I love you so much, Megan." Jesse gave her another long kiss. A quiet sniffle from behind interrupted them. Jesse glanced down to see Seana swiping at her eyes.

"Hey, what's the matter?" He ruffled her hair. "You're going to be an aunt. Don't you like the idea?" Seana shrugged.

"What else did Tess say, Seana?" Megan lifted her sister's chin. "What did she tell you?"

Seana tried to turn away. A tear trickled down her cheek. "She. . .she said you won't want me around anymore and will probably put me in an orphanage since Momma and Papa died."

Megan gasped. "That's the craziest thing I've ever heard. Why would we want to get rid of you?"

"Because I don't belong to you. I'm only a sister. Tess says you'll only want your children around you now." Seana's lower lip quivered. Megan's mouth opened and closed as if she were so shocked she couldn't think of anything to say.

Jesse turned farther on the seat. "Seana, do you understand what it means to be an aunt?" Seana shook her head, looking as miserable as a child could.

"Well, I know something about it because I'm an uncle." He waited until Seana gazed up at him, a glimmer of hope in her expression. "My sisters both have children, and while I lived back home, I often went over to play with them. I took the older ones fishing or hunting. I even escorted my oldest niece to a church social. She wanted to go with a boy and her parents agreed she was too young for such a thing. I volunteered to take her, and everyone was happy with that. We had a wonderful time.

"As our child's aunt, you will have the responsibility of loving the baby and helping to guide her as she grows up. You can teach her games and show her how to do different jobs."

"Ahem." Megan tapped him on the chest with her finger. "What if this baby is a boy?"

Jesse grinned. "Then she'll help show *him* how to do things." He looked back at Seana, whose face had lit up. He could see she was considering how important her job would be.

"Does Sally like her baby brother?" Megan asked.

Seana nodded. "She likes them all most of the time. She says it's fun to have someone to play with or to dress up like a doll."

"See?" Megan smoothed some flyaway hair from Seana's forehead. "You'll have fun with this baby, too."

Seana wrapped her arms around her legs and gazed off into the distance. Jesse could almost read her thoughts. She loved playing with Ennis, and this baby would be one more doll to attend to. Turning back around, he drew Megan close for a brief hug before continuing on to town. A father. The thought filled him with awe, fear, and joy all at the same time.

As they drew closer to town, Jesse could sense Megan tensing. She still hated coming to town, although she seemed to be enjoying the church services and the fellowship they had with those who attended. Jesse knew she still felt uncomfortable around the reverend and Mr. Sparks. Today they would be facing Mr. Sparks at the bank.

Jesse had finished the early planting. Despite all the chores that still needed doing, he and Megan couldn't afford to wait any longer before talking with the banker. There had to be some way to extend the loan until fall, when the crops would sell and they would have the money to pay the bank.

He would also need to go by the post office and see if his letter had been answered. William had asked last Sunday if he'd heard anything. Another family had been put out of their home by the bank. William knew them some and thought they had paid their loan. Just like many of the previous people, this family was there one day and gone the next. Something wasn't right, and Jesse intended to find out what.

Yankton appeared sleepy in the late morning. Most of the residents were working or at home preparing meals. The students whose families could spare them were at school; the other children worked alongside fathers and mothers in the fields and gardens. A light breeze took the heat from the sun, not making the air cold, but providing a freshness that felt good. The fresh scent of rain hung in the air from an early morning shower. Jesse drew in a deep breath, enjoying the smell.

He caught Megan's hand in his and held on, hoping to give her some support. Her face had paled as they reached town. Most likely she was nervous, but after the news shared on the road, he wondered if she was feeling sick again. He stopped the wagon in front of the bank.

"You okay?" Megan jumped as Jesse spoke close to her ear to keep Seana from hearing.

Her attempt at a smile didn't last. "I'll be fine."

Before Jesse could tie the horses, Seana had scrambled from the wagon. He helped Megan down, gave her a quick hug, and stepped back. "Ready?"

Megan took a deep breath, nodded, and lifted her chin.

Jesse grinned and held out his arm.

When they entered the bank, there was only one customer, an old man doing more talking than the teller seemed to want to hear. Mr. Sparks stepped from his office as the door closed behind them. He rocked back on his heels and patted his generous paunch. Jesse could feel the anger curling up inside him. Sparks had the look of a predatory animal about to pounce on its prey. Jesse knew he and Megan were the prey.

"Good afternoon, Mr. Coulter. Have you come to pay off that loan?" The smirk on Sparks's face told Jesse the man knew he wouldn't be able to come up with the money.

"No, Sir, but we would like to speak with you about the loan if you have the time." Jesse kept one hand on Megan. Seana stood behind them, subdued for the moment. The old man had ceased talking to the teller. The only sound in the bank was the ticking of the grandfather clock against the back wall.

"Come right on in." Sparks gestured at his office door. "Maybe we can make this transfer early and fast."

Jesse ignored the insinuation and guided Megan toward the office. He nodded at a chair along one wall, and Seana plopped down to wait for them. Sparks lumbered across the floor and settled into a protesting chair behind his desk. Jesse and Megan sat close together, a united front against the injustice of what Sparks had planned.

Opening a drawer, Sparks brought out some papers. He put them on the desktop and narrowed his eyes as he examined Jesse and Megan. "Well, are you ready to sign over the farm and admit you can't pay off the loan? That will save a lot of grief. If you do that, I'll even give you two weeks to pack up and move."

eighteen

Her fingers gripped the edge of the chair so hard, Megan wondered that the wood didn't crack. She wanted to scream. She wanted to throw something at this pompous windbag who thought he knew so much and had so much power. Her tongue refused to work. Bit by bit she calmed enough to ease her grip on the chair. The clock in the corner began to annoy her as each steady tick sounded like a stroke of thunder.

"My father did not have a loan with this bank, Mr. Sparks." Megan blinked in amazement at her controlled tone of voice. Ice crystals should have been sparkling in the air in front of her.

"I have the papers right here, Mrs. Coulter. I'm sure your parents didn't share such privileged information with you." Sparks riffled the incriminating papers with his meaty fingers.

"We found no papers or notes of any sort when we went through my parents' things. My father always kept perfect records of everything. Why would he not have an account of something like this loan when it meant he could lose the farm?"

"I can't answer that, Mrs. Coulter, and I'm afraid it's too late to ask your father."

Megan gasped. The blood drained from her face, leaving her light-headed. How could the man be so cruel?

"I'd like to see those papers." Jesse stood, stretching out his hand to the banker. Megan could see the ticking muscle in his jaw, the only indication of the anger he must feel.

"These are private records for the bank only, Mr. Coulter. I can't allow you to see them." Mr. Sparks opened the drawer and slipped the evidence out of sight.

"I believe when I married Megan, I became the owner of her father's farm. You consider me in charge of paying off the loan. Why won't you allow me to see the agreement you had with Mr. Riley?"

"You can take my word for what is written there. That's all you need." Sparks's chair creaked in protest as he leaned back. "All you need to do is come up with the money or sign the farm over. Which is it?"

A muscle in Jesse's jaw jumped. "Due to the rough winter and the death of Megan's parents, I'd like to ask you for an extension on the loan. We could pay you back in the fall when the crops come in."

"I'm afraid I can't do that." Mr. Sparks frowned. "If I let one person have an extension, then everyone will want one. It's bad for business."

"Mr. Sparks, my father is a banker. I've worked with him for years. You can't fool me." Jesse's eyes flashed. "I know you can hold off on payments without being hurt. An honest banker wouldn't withhold information or force people off the land when they've had such a difficult time."

Sparks stiffened. His eyes narrowed. "Maybe out here in the Territories we do things differently than you do in the big city, Mr. Coulter." He leaned forward, his meaty hands spread on the top of his desk. "I don't like your accusations. Because of Megan's difficulties, I will extend the loan for two weeks. That will give you six more weeks to come up with the money. On that day I will be at the farm and you will either pay me or be ready to leave."

He stood and gestured at the door. "I don't think we have any more to say to one another."

Stunned, Megan didn't think her legs would carry her from the office. She was going to lose her home. All the memories of her parents and brother, all the good times they shared were still there in that house and the land. She couldn't leave.

She felt a hand grip her elbow. As if in a dream, Megan looked down to find Jesse's strong fingers lifting her up. She didn't want to leave. There had to be some way to convince Mr. Sparks to let them have more time. They just couldn't lose their home. Where would they go?

Jesse let go of her elbow and gently touched her waist. He held her close like he was trying to shelter her from hurt. Her heart swelled with love for this man. What had her mother said when they left their home to move to Dakota Territory? Home is not a place, but a group of people. As long as she had Jesse, Seana, and now the baby, she would be at home. Her memories of her family would always be there, no matter where Jesse took them to live.

As they stepped out onto the street, the sun dipped behind a cloud, bathing everything in shade for a few minutes. Down the street a man carried a child into the doctor's house. The sheriff stood in front of the jail, an imposing figure even from this distance. A man hurried along the walkway, most likely heading home for his lunch. Megan thought life seemed to go on for others no matter how the current crises made her feel as if time were at a standstill.

"I need to check on some mail." Jesse managed to give her cheek a chaste kiss as he spoke close to her ear. "Do you want to go with me or wait in the wagon? As soon as I get done, we'll head home."

"Seana and I will wait for you." Megan forced herself to move closer to their horses. "I don't want to sit down. We'll be doing enough of that on the trip home."

Jesse gave her arm a light squeeze. "Okay. I'll be back as soon as I can. This shouldn't take long."

Time seemed to stretch as Megan and Seana walked a bit, then stood by the wagon. The sun played peekaboo with clouds that were growing larger and darker. Megan pushed away the worry that they would be caught out in a storm on the way home. She hated for Seana to be exposed to weather like that. Her sister had been getting stronger and hadn't been sick for weeks now. She didn't want that to change.

"Ready to go?"

Megan jumped as Jesse spoke from behind her. She hadn't heard or seen him coming. One glance at the frown on his face told her his news hadn't been good. She could see at least two letters protruding from his pocket. With his help, she climbed aboard the wagon, trying to wait patiently for him to tell her what he'd heard.

They rode in silence for the first hour. Seana, tired from the long morning trip, lay down in the wagon bed and took a nap. Megan wished she could join her sister. The past couple of weeks she'd been so tired. A thrill flowed through her as she remembered the cause of her unusual exhaustion. She would be having a baby this winter. From her reckoning, the little one should arrive around Thanksgiving or Christmastime.

In the midst of plans for making baby clothes, knitting stockings and such, Megan didn't realize Jesse had been talking until he touched her arm. She jumped. "I'm sorry, did you say something?"

"Were you asleep or doing some heavy thinking?" A slight smile let her know he wasn't upset with her.

Her faced warmed. "I. . .I was thinking about the baby." She stared down at her feet, not sure why she was so embarrassed.

Jesse slipped his arm around her shoulder. "I haven't gotten used to the idea of me being a father, but I am happy." He paused, his fingers caressing her arm. "In fact, I haven't been this content before in my life. I know the situation with the bank looks grim, but I can't help feeling as if I'm right where God wants me to be. Does that make sense?"

Megan's vision blurred. She blinked as she gazed up into Jesse's serious face. Staring into his eyes, she thought she could see into the very depths of his soul. Emotion welled up, almost choking her. *Jesus, You blessed me so much with this man. Thank You.*

"It makes perfect sense." Megan touched Jesse's cheek. "I do get afraid sometimes, but right now I'm looking forward to seeing how God will work this out. After all, He's the one who got you to start the church out here. I don't believe He'll ask us to quit before we truly get started."

Jesse hugged her close, a slight smile easing his serious expression. "I need to talk to you about something." Thunder rumbled in the distance. Jesse flicked the reins to urge the horses to keep moving. Megan knew this had something to do with the letters he'd gotten. She tried to relax, but had the feeling bad news would follow.

"I need to leave." Jesse's arm tightened as Megan flinched.

"What?" She pushed away from him, half-turning so she could see him better.

"I have to go back home. I have some business there." He touched the envelopes protruding from his pocket. "My father is very sick."

Megan gasped. "I'm sorry. Of course, you'll want to go."

"Thank you for understanding. While I'm there, I also need to attend to some matters I've been looking into." Jesse dwarfed her small hand with his large one and gave a comforting squeeze. "This is a bad time for me to be gone, but I'll get back as fast as I can. At least I won't have any blizzards to contend with this time." His attempt to lighten the moment failed.

"How long will it take you to ride all the way to Chicago and back?" Megan tried to act like she wasn't scared.

"I'm not going to ride there. William suggested I go to Sioux Falls and take the train. That way my travel time will be cut. I'm hoping to be back in two weeks at the most. Sparks gave us six weeks, so I'll be here in plenty of time to keep him away."

"Keep him away? William suggested the train?" Megan

shook her head, feeling like there must be cobwebs keeping her from thinking straight. "I think maybe you should explain what you're talking about."

Raindrops spattered around them. Jesse reached back and wrestled the tarp over the edges of the wagon so Seana wouldn't get wet. Then he pulled a smaller piece over Megan and himself for shelter.

"William and I have been talking about the problems with the bank. We have some ideas that something isn't right. I think I know why. I had planned to go back east soon anyway, depending on what I heard after I wrote to my father." He gave Megan a cocky grin. "I have a plan for saving our farm, but I really wanted to surprise you. What I have in mind may not work. Will you trust me?"

Gazing into his love-filled eyes, Megan couldn't do anything else.

❧

Jesse stared out the window as the train chugged into the station. People hurried every which way, trying to find the right person or the right train. Porters stood by piles of suitcases. For the past few miles, all Jesse had seen were buildings, houses, and people. How he missed the wide-open spaces and rolling hills back home. He smiled. Already this place felt foreign, and his heart longed to be back with his real family.

Joining the line of people inching their way off the train, Jesse prayed as he had most of the trip here. He wanted so much for his plan to work out, but more than that, he wanted to be in God's will. The upcoming confrontation with his family wouldn't be pleasant. He needed to be firm, but loving. What did the Bible say? "Wise as serpents, and harmless as doves?" That's what he would have to become and that would only happen with God's help.

"Jesse. Jesse. Over here."

Glancing around, Jesse could see the arm waving over the

crowd. One of his sisters must have come to greet him. He'd sent a telegram letting them know what train he would arrive on. The throng parted. Instead of his sister, Jesse stood face-to-face with Sara, his ex-fiancée. She threw her arms around his neck, kissing his cheek with enthusiasm.

"Oh, Jesse, I missed you so much. I can't believe you're home." She leaned back a little to bat her impossibly blue eyes at him. "I begged Amanda to let me be the one to meet you. I wanted it to be a surprise, though. Surprised?" Her beauty hadn't diminished, but her effect on him had. Jesse let his satchel drop, removed her arms from around his neck, and gave her a gentle push.

"Now look at me." Sara laughed, her eyes sparkling, her cheeks flushed. "Here we are in the middle of a train station, and I'm throwing myself at you. I'm surprised you weren't so embarrassed you jumped right back on that train." In a swirl of skirts, she turned and wrapped her arm through his, standing so close a curl of her long, red-gold hair rested on his shoulder. "I didn't mean to overwhelm you. I just missed you so much."

"Sara, that's enough." Jesse stepped aside, loosening her arm. "Didn't Amanda tell you I'm married?"

Sara waved one hand in the air. "Oh, that. She said something about you thinking you were married to some country bumpkin. Don't worry, Amanda's husband already has the legalities figured out. You'll be free in no time. Then you and I can continue with our wedding plans."

"I have no such intentions of getting out of my marriage. My wife and I are expecting a baby."

Sara paled and took a step back. Her gaze narrowed. Jesse remembered how she didn't like to have her plans changed or thwarted. With a sharp snap, she flipped open a fan and began to wave it in front of her face. She gave him a dazzling smile, one designed to render men speechless. "Come along. Let's get you home and your father can try to talk some sense into you."

"I thought my father was extremely ill."

"He may be sick, but he's not dead." Sara grabbed his arm, ushering him away from the platform and out to the line of carriages. "Come along, your family is waiting."

The ride to his house seemed interminable. Jesse sat as far from Sara as he could, but she ignored his discomfort as she repeatedly brushed her fingers across his hand or arm as she pointed out ways the city had changed in the months since he'd been gone.

At the house, Jesse's mother seemed to be the only one eager to see him. His sisters and their husbands maintained a cool attitude, as if his return wasn't at all welcome. His nieces and nephews, busy with their games, greeted him, then dashed away.

"Your father is in the bedroom." Jesse's mother drew him into the parlor away from the rest. "He isn't as strong as he used to be, Jesse. Try not to upset him. The doctor says his heart can't stand the strain anymore." She smiled and patted his hand. "He's better, though. As soon as he heard you were coming home, he began making wedding plans for you and Sara. He even has a surprise or two for you that he wants to announce tonight."

The bedroom door swung open soundlessly. His father, seated in a comfortable chair, surrounded by pillows and blankets, looked as gray as a blizzard sky. Jesse knew without any doctor's learned opinion that his father was dying. His father roused up, peering at Jesse, his gaze probing and intense as always.

"Jesse, you've finally come. I always knew you would come to your senses and return home to take up the business before I die." He indicated a chair near his. "Sit down. Let's plan your return to the bank and your wedding."

nineteen

Sleep evaded Jesse again. His bare feet made little noise as he padded down the hallway to his father's room. Two weeks had passed since he left home. Part of him longed to be back with Megan and Seana, yet another part needed to be here with his dying father. Although they disagreed on so much, Jesse didn't want to give up the hope that he could lead his father to a true knowledge of Jesus Christ before he died. He couldn't bear the thought of his father not having the chance to go to heaven.

The hinge gave a slight squeak as he eased the door open. A lamp turned low cast the room in a shadowy light. Jenkins, his father's butler, sat in a chair close to the bed, his light snores telling Jesse he was asleep. In the past few days, his father had grown noticeably weaker. The whole family knew he didn't have long to live.

"Jenkins."

The butler jerked awake at Jesse's whisper and light touch on his shoulder.

"Go to bed. I'll sit with him until morning."

"But, Sir, you have the meetings at the bank in the morning." Jenkins held himself ramrod straight. "I'm sorry I fell asleep. It won't happen again."

"Jenkins, you've done enough." Jesse clapped his hand on the man's shoulder. "I can't sleep. I'll be fine. Go on to bed."

For a moment Jesse thought Jenkins would protest again. He could see the indecision warring within the man. With a quick nod, Jenkins glanced once more at his employer, then marched from the room. Jesse watched until the door closed, then moved the chair closer to the bed. Throughout the exchange, his father hadn't stirred. Only the shallow rise and fall of his chest showed any life in him.

His silent vigil gave Jesse plenty of time to think and pray about the upcoming days. So far, his time at home hadn't gone as planned—not his plan or his father's. The major upheaval had been over his marriage to Megan. His parents insisted on an annulment, saying he'd been railroaded into marrying the girl. They didn't understand his explanation of God's design and that all the events in his life were working according to what God wanted for him. Refusing to agree to an annulment brought his father's ire and his mother's tears, but Jesse stood firm.

He'd found the information he needed, but couldn't leave as long as his father was so sick and the bank was in turmoil. For the past week, Jesse had been meeting with his brothers-in-law and the other officials at the bank, trying to get the paperwork done to transfer the leadership. His father wanted him to become head of the bank, but Jesse had no interest in doing so. He wanted to return to his family, his farm, and the church the Lord called him to start. Several times he and his father had spoken on the subject. Jesse assured him that his brothers-in-law were very capable of managing the business. To his father, their years of experience were nothing compared to his desire to have his only son inherit everything.

Jesse's thoughts turned to Megan. He never dreamed he would miss her so much after the short time they'd been married. The last five months had been the best of his life, despite the pneumonia. He grinned. Maybe because of the pneumonia. He knew that wasn't true. For the first time in his life, he was trying to follow Jesus in every way. Because of that, he'd been blessed with the woman of his dreams. Life might not always be easy and there were sure to be plenty of rough spots ahead, but he looked forward to living through everything with Megan beside him.

Every day Jesse wondered if he would get a letter from Megan. He'd written to her twice to let her know about his father and the situation with the bank. Before he left Dakota Territory, he'd made arrangements with William to check on the mail when he was in town and deliver anything that came for Megan.

His father groaned. Jesse raised the wick on the lamp as he leaned over the bed. Something had changed. His father's breathing sounded more labored; his color didn't look as good.

"Jesse." Richard Coulter's fingers felt like claws as they gripped Jesse's hand.

"I'm right here." Jesse touched his father's forehead, wiping away a film of perspiration. "Let me send for the doctor."

"No." The forcefulness of the word seemed to cost his father strength. He panted for a moment, but didn't let go of Jesse. "I want to talk with you. Must talk."

"What is it?"

"The papers. Are they done?"

"Yes. You signed the last of the papers today. At tomorrow's meeting your sons-in-law will take over the bank. Mother has been provided for, as have all your grandchildren. You can relax and not worry about a thing."

"You?" His father coughed and grimaced in pain.

"I'll always be on the board at the bank. Everything has been arranged as per your instructions."

His father's eyes seemed to clear. "It's time, Jesse."

A knot formed in Jesse's throat. As much as he and his father disagreed on almost everything, he didn't want to lose him, either. "Let me go get Mother. I'll send Jenkins for the doctor."

"No." His father's grip held. "Talk first."

"What do you want to talk about?"

"Is it true? What you believe?"

Jesse's heart leaped. "You mean about Jesus? About His

dying for us so we have a way to heaven?" His father nodded. "Every word I read to you from the Bible the other day is true. Jesus paid the price for your sins and mine so we would have eternal life with Him."

"I've thought a lot about what you said. I think you may be right."

Jesse knew what those words cost his father. Richard Coulter had never been a man to admit to anyone else being right when it meant he might be wrong about something. The Holy Spirit must have been working on his heart to bring him to this point.

"Go get your mother while I spend some time alone."

As his father released him, Jesse stood. Two days ago he'd explained to his father how to accept Jesus as Savior. *Please, God, help him to be able to humble himself. Help me to know, too, Lord, please.*

ॐ

"Megan." Seana's cry was almost drowned out by the crashing of the door as she flung it open. "Megan, Mama Kitty, come quick." Tears tracked down Seana's cheeks as she grabbed Megan's hand and lunged back toward the door.

"Seana, stop. What's wrong?"

"It's Mama Kitty. She's hurt. You've got to help her." Seana swiped at her cheek with the back of her hand, leaving a dirty smear.

"Let me dry my hands." Megan wiped the water from her hands and hurried out the door after her sister. Seana flew to the barn, not slowing as she ran inside. Dread filled Megan as she saw the still body lying in a pile of hay. Mama Kitty had been missing since last night. Her newborn kittens were crying, most likely so hungry they were getting weak by now. Megan dropped down beside Seana.

"Seana, I'm sorry, there's nothing we can do for her." Megan blinked back tears.

"But the babies. They need their mama. How will they eat?" Seana's shoulders bowed as if she carried the weight of the world.

Wrapping her arm around her sister's shoulders, Megan tried to comfort her. "I don't know what to do, Seana. It looks like Mama Kitty was attacked. She managed to crawl back here, but she didn't live." Megan fell silent as Shadow, their other mother cat, slunk forward to sniff at Mama Kitty's body. The feeble cries of the kittens scraped at her nerves.

"Seana, let's pray. The Bible says God even knows when a sparrow falls, so He cares about these kittens. Let's pray for them." Megan took Seana's hand and waited for her sister to bow her head. "Jesus, You know how these little ones needed their mother. We're asking You to provide the help they have to have to survive since their Mama Kitty died. Please, help them. Help us, too, Lord."

Seana sniffled. For the past few days she'd been out in the barn every chance she could get free to see the baby kittens. She would watch them for hours. Shadow had kittens, too, but she wasn't as tame and would move them every time Seana found them.

"Seana, look." Megan nodded her head at Shadow. The cat had backed away from Mama Kitty and was staring at the place where the kittens were huddled in a writhing ball.

"Is she going to hurt them?" Seana whispered.

"I don't think so." Megan wasn't sure what the cat would do. Shadow inched closer to the yowling babies. She stopped and glanced back over her shoulder at Mama Kitty, as if trying to decide what to do. Taking another step, she leaned close and sniffed at the kittens. Their cries became more fervent, like they were begging for food from this stranger. With one more backward look, Shadow climbed in with the orphans. Making small comforting mews, she lay down and began to nudge and lick them as they sought the nourishment they needed.

As quiet settled over the barn, Seana turned to look at Megan, her eyes wide. "Shadow is feeding them. Do you think God sent her to help Mama Kitty's babies?"

"I sure do." Megan hugged her sister. "God has a way of knowing our needs and providing for them."

Seana turned back to watch the little ones nurse. "Just like God sent Jesse to us."

Megan tightened her hold on Seana's shoulders. She couldn't speak for a moment. "That's right. When we lost Momma, Papa, and Matt, God already had Jesse there to help us. God always watches out for us, Seana."

"I still miss them." Seana's voice trembled, but she didn't sound angry, only sad.

"I miss them, too. That's all right."

They sat quiet for several minutes, watching the miracle before them. Megan's legs began to ache. She stood and brushed the hay and bits of dirt from her skirt. "Come on, you can help me bury Mama Kitty. Then we'll fix supper together."

As Megan picked up the shovel, Seana stopped her. "I'm sorry I was so mean to Jesse. I do like him. I wish he would come home."

Megan hugged her again. "I know. Four weeks is a long time."

As they walked out of the barn, William rode into the yard. He waved an envelope at Megan. "I had to go to town today. I picked this up for you." He handed her the letter. "Sorry I didn't get there sooner. You doing all right?"

"We're fine, Mr. Bright. How are Edith and the children?"

"They're fine, except for that little one. He's getting some teeth and is fussier than a runt piglet." He tipped his hat. "I've got to get on home and do the chores."

"Can we get you something to eat or drink before you go?" Megan was torn between wanting to be neighborly and wanting to read her letter. She hoped this would be word from

Jesse saying when he would be home.

"No, thanks, but we'll be seeing you on Sunday. Edith and the young 'uns sure do look forward to worshiping together."

"We'll see you then." Megan waved as William's big roan cantered from the yard. Glancing at the envelope, she felt disappointment that the handwriting wasn't Jesse's. The neat letters looked like a more feminine hand. Shading her eyes to look at the sun, she stuffed the missive in her pocket. Reading this would have to wait until chores were done.

She didn't remember the letter until Seana was already asleep. Megan sank into the rocking chair to relax a moment before heading for bed. The crinkle of paper reminded her, and she brought the envelope from her pocket. Turning the lamp up, Megan still had to squint to read the fine writing.

> *Dear Megan,*
>
> *My brother, Jesse Coulter, asked me to write to you and inform you that he won't be returning to Dakota Territory. He apologizes for any inconvenience this causes you. He has many obligations here at home and will be staying to run the family business. Due to the unusual nature of your marriage, he's been advised to apply for an annulment. The papers will be coming to you as soon as possible, and you will be free to remarry.*
>
>

Sincerely,

Amanda Coulter Bradley
>

Megan couldn't breathe. Her chest felt as if she would explode from the hurt. Jesse wasn't coming back. He was leaving her, Seana, and the baby. Deep down she'd always known this would happen. How could a girl like her attract someone like Jesse? Oh, how she loved him, but she understood, too. His family, and probably the girl he'd been engaged to, needed him more than she did.

Crumpling the letter in a ball, she thrust it into her pocket. In a haze, she went about her bedtime ritual: checking Seana, blowing out the lamps, making sure things were ready for morning. After closing the bedroom door, Megan flung herself on the bed, still in her clothes, and cried until the covers were soaked. She'd never hurt so much in her life. What would they do? She and Seana couldn't hope to pay the loan. They would be thrown off the land, and she could picture Mr. Sparks smirking as he watched them leave. Where would they go?

Oh, Jesus, help us. You will have to perform a miracle for us to stay here. Help me to not worry, but to leave everything to You, Lord. She hesitated a moment. *And, Lord, please watch over Jesse. You know how much I love him. No matter what he's done, I still love him.*

She fell asleep and dreamed of being in a green pasture. The flowers smelled sweet, the grass was like a thick carpet. She lay there with her head on Jesus' lap as He stroked her hair and told her everything would be according to His plan. The morning sun peeking in the windows woke her. Megan sat up and stretched, surprised to feel so refreshed and content. She had no idea how, but she knew Jesus would bring them through this.

Megan worked hard, hoping the effort would keep her from dwelling on her problems. After all, she reminded herself time and again, these weren't her worries, but the Lord's. He could take care of anything.

"Megan, someone's coming." Seana stumbled into the house, her face flushed, eyes shining with excitement.

Following her sister out the door, Megan shaded her eyes, trying to see the approaching visitors against the late morning sun. One drove in a buggy, the other on a horse. Her heart sank as she recognized the sheriff and Mr. Sparks.

"Good morning, Mrs. Coulter." Mr. Sparks began to talk before he even had the buggy stopped. "Have you got the payment for the loan? This is the first of June."

"You gave us a two-week extension. We came to the bank and talked to you about it." A surprising calm enveloped Megan.

"Yes, well, I don't believe we have any paperwork to that effect, do we?" Sparks heaved his bulk from the buggy. The sheriff swung down from his horse and stood behind the banker. Mr. Sparks stepped forward. "Have you got the money?"

"No, I don't." Megan drew herself up tall.

Mr. Sparks leered at her. "Where is this husband of yours?"

"He's gone back east. His father is very ill."

"That's too bad. Sounds to me like he left you when times got tough. You should have taken me up on my offer." Mr. Sparks chuckled. "Now, you'll have two hours to get the things you want and leave. The sheriff is here to see that you do go. We'll wait inside." He strode past Megan and Seana, entering the house like a king going into his castle.

twenty

"I don't want to leave here." Seana sniffed as she wrapped her clothes in a blanket to carry to the wagon.

"I don't want to leave, either, but we have no choice. We can't fight the sheriff on this. If we don't go, he'll arrest us. Then what will we do?" Megan tried to swallow around the lump in her throat. For the past hour, she and Seana had worked feverishly to pack what they could and load the wagon. Sheriff Armstrong offered to hitch the horses for her, but Megan refused his help. The man was guilty of helping Sparks throw families out of their homes. She didn't want him doing anything for her.

"I need to load that chair in the wagon." Megan tried hard to keep the disdain from her voice as she faced Mr. Sparks, sitting in her mother's rocker.

Sparks rubbed his fingers over the armrest, stroking the dark wood. "Why this is one of the nicest rockers I've ever sat in. I think I might like this chair to stay with the house."

Megan held her clenched fists tight against her sides. "You can't do that."

Narrowing his eyes, Sparks gave her a look intended to freeze her in place. "You have no idea what I can do. You should have married me. Then you wouldn't be in this predicament." He settled back in the chair and began to rock. "Of course, I know you're regretting your decision by now." His feral smile made her shudder.

"Why would I do that?"

"Because your new husband isn't planning to come back, is he?"

"How did you. . .?" Megan snapped her mouth shut.

Paper crumpled as Sparks dragged a wrinkled envelope from his pocket. Megan's hand slapped her apron where she'd stuffed the letter this morning. It was gone, fallen out when she hadn't noticed.

"That is private. Give it back." She held out her hand, trying to keep it from shaking. Seana came back in and stopped. She could probably feel the tension in the room and wondered what was going on. Megan gestured for her to leave, but Seana ignored her.

"I just found this lying on the floor. I couldn't be sure who it belonged to." Sparks smoothed open the paper. "Sounds to me like you'll be in the market for a new husband soon. Mr. Coulter seems to have found better prospects."

"No!" Seana raced across the room, flinging herself in Megan's arms. "He's lying. Jesse's coming back. He won't leave us and the baby."

Sparks's eyes widened. "Baby? Oh, this is interesting." He heaved his bulk up from the chair. "I intended to make you an offer again, but I won't take on another man's child. Your time is as good as up. You've loaded enough of your things. Sheriff, see that they leave."

"But they haven't finished packing." Sheriff Armstrong frowned. "They still have about an hour left to gather their belongings."

Sparks's face reddened. "I said their time is up. I pay you to obey my orders. Now get them out of here."

Megan could almost see the thoughts warring in the sheriff's head. If Sparks admitted to paying him to do this work, then the sheriff wasn't evicting them for legal reasons. Her mind raced as she tried to think of something to halt this travesty.

"Come on." Sheriff Armstrong gripped her arm and propelled her past the smirking banker to the door. "I'll help you in the wagon, then load your chair for you."

"How does it feel to be a pawn?" Anger welled up in Megan at the injustice. "I thought you took an oath to uphold the law, not to work for whoever could pay you the most money."

"Quiet!" Sheriff Armstrong jerked her arm as he stepped outside. His reddened face and narrowed gaze told her she should be quiet, but she was too angry to stop.

"Someday you'll have to answer for what you're doing here, for what you've done to all the people you've put off their land illegally."

"This isn't illegal. Sparks has papers saying you can't pay up on the loan your parents took out at the bank."

"My parents didn't take a loan out at the bank. They did not owe him any money. Those papers are forgeries. I'm sure of it."

"Are you saying our esteemed banker is doing something illegal here?"

"That's what she's saying, Sheriff." They both jerked around at the new voice. "And if you don't take your hands off my wife in the next two minutes, you'll be in more trouble than you can handle."

"Jesse." As the sheriff let go, Megan ran to her husband. He swung off his horse and pulled her into his embrace. The two men with him also dismounted.

"Jesse." Seana barreled into her sister and Jesse, laughing in delight.

"Hey, Seana, I missed you." Jesse leaned down and gave her a kiss on the forehead before straightening to face the sheriff and the banker. "I'd like to introduce you gentlemen to some new acquaintances of mine. This is Marshall Trumble and Mr. Owens, an auditor. They're here to check into the practices of the bank and the way people have been losing their land and homes."

Jesse's arm tightened around Megan. She rested her head against his shoulder. "It seems Mr. Sparks isn't really Mr. Sparks. He comes from back East, where he lived as Mr.

Wiggins, then as Mr. Burns. Marshall Trumble has been tracking him for some time. This isn't the first time he's forged papers and forced people out of their homes. He's good at copying signatures of people who have done business with him."

Marshall Trumble stepped forward. A big man, he looked like someone used to getting his way. "Wiggins, you thought you got away, didn't you? Well, you're coming with me. We're going over your bank records. If this place is like the last two, you've been skimming off these people's accounts, too. Mr. Owens will help us get it all sorted out."

Stunned, Megan watched the marshall escort Mr. Sparks to his buggy. Sheriff Armstrong followed, looking like a boy caught with his hand in the cookie jar. She guessed he would be accountable for helping with the fraud. Her heart was so full of thanksgiving, she couldn't say anything as she walked to the house with Seana and Jesse.

"What's this?" Jesse bent to pick up the letter his sister sent Megan. It lay in the dirt where Mr. Sparks must have dropped it. Jesse scanned the writing, his face darkening in anger. "I can't believe she did this." He crushed the letter in his hand. "Did you believe her?" Jesse turned Megan to face him.

"Mr. Bright brought the letter yesterday. I read it last night. Yes, I believed it at first, but after I prayed, I knew that everything would work out fine, and it has."

Jesse drew her to him. "Megan, I love you so much. All I could think of back there was coming home to be with you, Seana, and the baby. I wrote to you twice, but I gave the letters to Amanda to mail. I'm guessing she didn't send them."

Megan couldn't stop smiling. "I have you home. The letters don't matter that much."

epilogue

October 1888

A cacophony of sounds brightened the sunny fall day. Children laughed as they chased each other over the hills and around the new church building. Women chattered in excited voices as they set baskets of food on tables, ready to be opened and shared after the services. Men stood in groups discussing the weather, the harvest, or admiring the way the steeple of the church gleamed in the light.

Jesse thought his chest would burst as he stood at the top of the steps and watched the gathering. The last few months had been busy. He and William Bright agreed to donate a piece of property where their land joined for a church, which could also be used as a school. The women were thrilled, since they lived too far from town for their children to attend classes. The new schoolteacher should be arriving any day. The harvesting would be over soon, and the children would be free to come.

Megan moved among the women, comfortable in her role as pastor's wife. She loved greeting each one and was adept at finding out little ways to help each family. Her caring nature brought the women to her when they had problems or needed something. Megan always seemed willing to pray with them and offer what help she could. As her faith deepened, Jesse had come to depend on their discussions of Scripture. He didn't know how he lived so many years without her.

Running her hand over her bulging stomach, Megan glanced up at Jesse and sent him a brilliant smile. They were both anxious to become parents. Jesse didn't think a baby had ever been wanted more than this one. They spent hours talking about names and planning things to teach and do with the baby. Megan insisted that since the death of Jesse's father, they should take time to visit his mother after the baby came. She was careful to point out to him how important family would be to her.

"Jesse, can I ring the bell?" Seana hopped up the steps, her cheeks flushed with all the running she'd been doing. This summer had seen a change in her. Megan said her mother tended to keep Seana in the house, afraid the frail child would get sick and die from exposure to the elements. Jesse insisted she needed the exercise and allowed her outside except in the worst weather. He thought that was the reason she had filled out and looked so healthy now.

"Looks like everyone is here." Jesse ruffled Seana's wind-blown hair. "Go ahead and ring the bell. We'll get everyone in and see if the building stands up to our singing."

Seana laughed as she skipped through the church doors. Jesse nodded at Mr. Owens as the man tied his horse to the hitching rack. Mr. Owens had taken over the bank. Jesse helped him some with business matters he wasn't sure of, but it had taken the two of them weeks to straighten out the mess created by Sparks. The banker now resided in prison. Sheriff Armstrong insisted he was innocent and hadn't known what Sparks was doing. Payment records spoke differently. Sparks had kept meticulous records, which helped convict Armstrong to a lesser degree and returned many properties to their rightful owners.

The bell pealed, the sound rolling across the prairie. People began moving toward the church steps. Megan hurried to Jesse's side to help greet everyone as they entered. After they were all seated, Samuel Duncan led them in several songs. In the past months he'd lost his awkwardness and embarrassment.

Now he led the singing with an enthusiasm that often brought people to their feet.

Stepping up to the podium, Jesse gazed out over the congregation. He'd come to know and love these people. They welcomed him and Megan, eager to have a place to truly worship Jesus. Although not everyone agreed with every word he said, they agreed on the essentials of the gospel. The one thing he appreciated was that they were willing to talk with him about their disagreements rather than gossiping among themselves.

"I'd like for you to look in the book of Malachi with me, chapter 3, verses 16 through 18." Jesse waited for a minute until the sound of turning pages ceased. Not everyone had a Bible or knew how to read, but he encouraged those who could to bring their Bibles and follow along with him.

" 'Then they that feared the Lord spake often one to another: and the Lord hearkened, and heard it, and a book of remembrance was written before him for them that feared the Lord, and that thought upon his name. And they shall be mine, saith the Lord of hosts, in that day when I make up my jewels; and I will spare them, as a man spareth his own son that serveth him. Then shall ye return, and discern between the righteous and the wicked, between him that serveth God and him that serveth him not.' "

Every eye watched him. Jesse took a deep breath and began. "Every one of us has something precious that we value above our other possessions. I have my wife, Megan, our baby, and Seana. They are priceless to me. Today, I want to encourage each of you to remember that to God, you are a precious jewel. When you listen to what God has to say to you, and when you speak to one another of those things, when you fear Him and seek His will, then you will become one of God's gems. He can take what to others appears to be an ordinary rock and make something very special. I would like to see a whole church full to overflowing with jewels dedicated to following Jesus Christ."

As Jesse glanced down at his Bible, he couldn't help remembering how he'd run from God's call, yet Jesus had been faithful to draw him back. He could see Megan's shining face; and feeling the peace in his heart, he knew he was right where God wanted him.

A Letter To Our Readers

Dear Reader:

In order that we might better contribute to your reading enjoyment, we would appreciate your taking a few minutes to respond to the following questions. We welcome your comments and read each form and letter we receive. When completed, please return to the following:

Fiction Editor
Heartsong Presents
PO Box 719
Uhrichsville, Ohio 44683

1. Did you enjoy reading *Precious Jewels* by Nancy J. Farrier?
   ❑ Very much! I would like to see more books by this author!
   ❑ Moderately. I would have enjoyed it more if

   _____

   _____

   _____

2. Are you a member of **Heartsong Presents**? ❑ Yes ❑ No
   If no, where did you purchase this book? _____

   _____

3. How would you rate, on a scale from 1 (poor) to 5 (superior), the cover design? _____

4. On a scale from 1 (poor) to 10 (superior), please rate the following elements.

   ____ Heroine   ____ Plot
   ____ Hero   ____ Inspirational theme
   ____ Setting   ____ Secondary characters

6. How has this book inspired your life?_____
_____
_____

7. What settings would you like to see covered in future
   Heartsong Presents books? _____
   _____
   _____

8. What are some inspirational themes you would like to see
   treated in future books? _____
   _____
   _____

9. Would you be interested in reading other **Heartsong
   Presents** titles? ❏ Yes ❏ No

10. Please check your age range:
    ❏ Under 18   ❏ 18-24
    ❏ 25-34   ❏ 35-45
    ❏ 46-55   ❏ Over 55

Name_____
Occupation _____
Address _____
City_____ State_____ Zip_____
E-mail_____

Wildflower Brides

Thousands of hearty souls are traveling from Independence, Missouri, to the northwestern frontier along the Oregon Trail. Each is dreaming of a new life full of hope and prosperity.

Can four women find lasting romance among the dusty ruts of the Trail? Will hope in the stories of Trail's End—and faith in God's leading—get them over the mountains and settled into new lives?

Historical, paperback, 352 pages, 5 ³⁄₁₆" x 8"

Presents

Great Inspirational Romance at a Great Price!

Heartsong Presents books are inspirational romances in contemporary and historical settings, designed to give you an enjoyable, spirit-lifting reading experience. You can choose wonderfully written titles from some of today's best authors like Peggy Darty, Sally Laity, Tracie Peterson, Colleen L. Reece, Debra White Smith, and many others.

When ordering quantities less than twelve, above titles are $3.25 each.
Not all titles may be available at time of order.

*H*EARTSONG ❤ PRESENTS

Love Stories
Are Rated G!

That's for godly, gratifying, and of course, great! If you love a
thrilling love story but don't appreciate the sordidness of some
popular paperback romances, **Heartsong Presents** is for you. In
fact, **Heartsong Presents** is the only inspirational romance book
club featuring love stories where Christian faith is the primary
ingredient in a marriage relationship.

Sign up today to receive your first set of four, never-before-
published Christian romances. Send no money now; you will
receive a bill with the first shipment. You may cancel at any time
without obligation, and if you aren't completely satisfied with any
selection, you may return the books for an immediate refund!

Imagine. . .four new romances every four weeks—two historical, two contemporary—with men and women like you who long
to meet the one God has chosen as the love of their lives. . .all for
the low price of $10.99 postpaid.

To join, simply complete the coupon below and mail to the
address provided. **Heartsong Presents** romances are rated G for
another reason: They'll arrive Godspeed!

YES! Sign me up for Hearts❤ng!

NEW MEMBERSHIPS WILL BE SHIPPED IMMEDIATELY!
Send no money now. We'll bill you only $10.99 post-
paid with your first shipment of four books. Or for faster
action, call toll free 1-800-847-8270.

NAME _____

ADDRESS _____

CITY _____ STATE _____ ZIP _____

MAIL TO: HEARTSONG PRESENTS, P.O. Box 721, Uhrichsville, Ohio 44683
or visit www.heartsongpresents.com